BLISS

BLISS

A NOVEL

Jeff Lyon

Lori, Karen and I enjoyed your company at the wedding. May your life be filled with Bliss!

Jeff Lyon

5-14-18

ZONE PRESS
Denton, Texas

BLISS

By Jeff Lyon

Zone Press
an imprint of Rogers Publishing and Consulting, Inc.
109 East Oak – Suite 300
Denton, Texas 76201
info@zonepress.com

Jim O. Rogers - Editor
Charlotte Beckham - Copy Edit
Lori Walker - Production and Design
Jeff Lyon - Cover Design

Any resemblance to actual people and events is purely coincidental. This is a work of fiction.

Printed in the United States of America
ISBN:0-9761706-5-5

Thank-Yous

I would like to thank my editors, Donna Lyon and Helen Reneau. Their attention to details, hard work and encouragement were invaluable in making this book a polished composition. I would also like to express deep gratitude to my wife, Karen. Her unwavering support for all my endeavors makes them possible.

Government feeds off its people, is ever expanding and never shrinks. City Hall in Bliss was no exception.

CHAPTER 1
BLISS GROWS UP
◆◆◆

Bliss was a sleepy little farming town located a safe but accessible distance north of the sins and iniquities associated with a big city like Dallas. Bliss was a place you drove through on your way to somewhere else. Then a steady influx of commuters began moving their families to Bliss where they could afford bigger houses on bigger lots than in cramped Dallas. Parents wanted to raise their children in the relative security of this tiny hamlet and experience its easygoing lifestyle with a rural flavor. The land started out cheap, the people were friendly and living was good.

Along with the migration of the masses came their constantly increasing needs. Building more sewer lines to carry away their flushables resulted in a bigger pookey plant to deal with them at the other end. More water lines were needed to keep all those newly sodded lawns green and a bigger water plant was needed to deliver the goods. More cars would necessitate wider roads and better lighting. More leisure time away from the stresses of the Metroplex would require more parks and recreational facilities. More of this and more of that would continue to be added until Bliss grew into the very place all the new residents were running away from.

City government blossomed right along with all the unbridled growth of public amenities and new businesses. Government feeds off its people, is ever expanding and never shrinks. City Hall in Bliss was no exception.

I entered the picture at the dawn of the building boom in the mid 80s. That building boom never really ended and managed to blur the lines between Dallas and its northern suburbs all the way to the Oklahoma border.

I began my city career in the Bliss Health Department, which was located in a historic, two-cell jailhouse in the part of the city called "Old Town." There was a Chief Health Inspector, two regular Health Inspectors and a shared secretary in our tiny, red brick building.

On Tuesdays and Thursdays the County Health Department sent registered nurses to vaccinate children in our building. They administered shots required for children to attend public schools for a fraction of the price being charged by family doctors.

Long lines would form out the front door and down the street as the beginning of each new school year approached. The faces of happy, smiling kids who had been playing together in front of the building would cloud over with apprehension when they entered the building's miniscule reception area only to be confronted with screaming, crying children who had been freshly needle stabbed being dragged down the hallway and out the rear exit. I gladly vacated my office for the duration of these bi-weekly events.

Sharing parking on the same lot with the Health Department was City Hall, The Library and a Fire Station. By the end of the

80s, a huge new Civic Center would be constructed across town on Main Street with lots and lots more tax-consuming employees to staff it. In ten short years Bliss would attract big businesses and the population would swell from twenty-five to sixty thousand inhabitants. Rampant growth was a living thing that was going to happen with or without City Hall's stamp of approval.

Ms. Beaula Irons was running the show from that old City Hall before the big move to the shiny new structure across town. She demanded complete loyalty from her city employees and they got the same in return from her. Ms. Beaula governed in the classic "good ole boy" style where deals were done over breakfast at the local Eggs & More eatery and reports were given orally from Department Heads and regular staff in her open-door office. Nobody crossed Ms. Beaula and got away with it. She could make or break your project or career with a whisper and smile while you and your dreams faded out of the picture.

Ms. Beaula succumbed to cancer, which was the only thing in Bliss that wasn't afraid to disagree with her. Bliss hired a new city manager from a blossoming municipality on the eastern seaboard who came to town to promote growth and build bigger government. His name was Dick Darling and his managing style could not have been farther from Ms. Beaula's.

Dick added upper layers to all the city departments and only chiefs were privy to his company. Reports would all be written and then rewritten until Dick was happy with them and Bliss City Council members could easily grasp their gist. There was a new boss in town and he had no time for the minutia of day-to-day routines that occupied the time of city workers at the lower end of the pay scale. Department heads were expected to take care of petty problems before they reached Dick's ears or pay the price for failure.

The "Big Belly Boys" who had operated one-man departments became Department Heads with real staff numbers and were thrown into the game with out-of-town professionals to sink or swim. The new Civic Center meeting rooms filled with uncomfortable "good ole boys" in new ties, dress shirts and suits pitted against corporate expansion pros looking for cheap land and easy access to the Dallas/Fort Worth Airport. Egos got bruised and the learning curve shot straight up as many of the old school administrators were forced to dig through parts of the codes and ordinances they'd adopted but never read to come up with answers for eager developers. City slickers faced off with small town yokels, and the subsequent song and dance was a wrestling match with a liberal dose of smoke and mirrors. It was an ostentatious display and quite entertaining.

When the day came to move into the new Civic Center the word came down the line that each department was expected to move its own files to the new building. We would do this on a Saturday and like it. A lot of feathers were ruffled and the grumbling on moving day was not eased when those of us who had occupied our own offices in older buildings found ourselves elbow-to-elbow in cubicles outside our Department Head's spacious new offices. There was dissension among the ranks that were promptly told they could hit the bricks if they didn't get with the new program. Nobody quit.

Those heady days of explosive expansion have provided me with the grist for many humorous tales. My accidental career in city government was a hoot. Back we go to those innocent times when heading to jail in the morning meant working for the Bliss Health Department.

*All I had to do was take six weeks of classes, pass the state
exam and the next thing you know I'm a Registered Health
Inspector with the State of Texas*

CHAPTER 2
I NEVER INTENDED TO BE A HEALTH INSPECTOR

I attended college a few miles up the road from Bliss in the late 70s. My folks lived on the edge of Dallas, and Bliss was just a crossroads with a smattering of car lots and filling stations on my way home to get laundry done on weekends. Bliss certainly held no attraction for a college-age raconteur.

Few things stir pride in a father's heart like the announcement by his freshly graduated son that he is taking his spanking new degree to Colorado to be a ski-bum for a season. That ski season turned into four years and a volume of misadventures unto itself. A visiting buddy persuaded me that it was time to get a real job and give up the mountain mischief that had become my way of life. I took a hard look at the "lifer ski-bums" around me and decided he was right.

My buddy worked for one of those massive package delivery companies. He was doing quite well and would see about getting me a job. A great deal of correspondence and phone conversations later I was back in the Dallas area to start a genuine career. For reasons that still elude me a youthful indiscretion that I had been forthright and open about from the very beginning with all the people involved with my prospective employment suddenly became an insurmountable problem just days before I was to start my new job. After moving 900 miles with the lack of savings you would expect a ski-bum to possess, there would be no job delivering the world's packages door-to-door for me.

Another college chum, Bruce Manns, got wind of my plight and called to say that he was working for the City of Bliss and they had an opening in the Health Department for the summer season. The pay was not great, but it would tide me over while I continued the quest for the ever-illusive real job.

Bruce set up an interview with the Chief Health Inspector, Rex Flint, and I drove to Bliss to meet my new boss. Pam Hayes, the real head of the Health Department and Rex's secretary, greeted me inside the miniscule jail's door. Pam was grandmotherly at first blush, but I learned quickly that crossing her was a mistake. Pam looked up from her pile of immunization forms, smiled and said, "You must be Ross. Get yourself a cup of coffee and have a seat. Mr. Flint will be with you in a minute."

I went into the first room down the hall she had pointed to and got my initial taste of Health Department sludge. Rex Flint was a chain smoking, non-stop coffee drinker and the pot was left on all day. It was now early afternoon and I was sure the foam cup I poured the viscous elixir into would disintegrate on contact with the hot muck. I was looking for a plant or sink to pour it in when Rex entered to fill his cup.

Rex looked disappointed at the meager amount of coffee left stewing in the pot, but he drained it into his stained cup and said, "Pam, we need more coffee."

He turned to leave, stopped, looked back at me and asked, "Are you my two-o'clock?"

I replied, "I'm Ross Ryan, if that's your two-o'clock."

Rex put his cigarette in his mouth, shifted his coffee cup to his left hand and stuck out his right hand to shake mine. Through a cloud of exhaled smoke he mumbled, "Glad to meet you. Let's go in my office and talk."

Rex's office had no windows and the walls were covered with cheap, dark wood paneling. His desk barely fit across the far wall and two plastic chairs had been squeezed in front of it. It was like walking into a large ashtray. The light fixture and ceiling above his head had yellowed from years of rising smoke. He chain-smoked throughout my brief interview and made me close the door when I entered his dungeon.

Pointing at the sturdier of the two chairs Rex said, "Have a seat."

I sat down and handed him my resume. He looked it over pausing to look up at me from time to time and then tossed it into the heaping piles on his cluttered desk.

Rex took a huge drag on his cigarette and exhaled while asking me, "So why do you want to work for the Bliss Health Department?"

My eyes watered as I replied, "Because I need a job."

Rex took another drag and said; "You realize this is just a part-time job for the grass and weeds season?"

I had no idea what the grass and weeds season meant, but I needed work and the money so I replied, "Yes. I'm just looking for something to tide me over until I can find more permanent employment."

Rex thought for a minute, blew out an astonishing amount of smoke and said, "Well, you're overqualified for this position, but Bruce said you were a good man and I need someone to start next week. You're hired. See Pam about your paperwork and come in Monday."

I stood quickly, shook Rex's hand and bolted for the closed door in hopes of finding breathable air on the other side. Pam had just lit up a cigarette of her own and the little entry room closed in on me as I filled out the stack of forms to become a Bliss city employee.

My new job was to drive around town in an unmarked cruiser that had been cast-off by the police department and send letters to people who were in violation of the city's ordinances pertaining to grass and weeds, unsightly material and inoperative vehicles. I had become the mom for an entire city. "Clean that up now and I mean it!"

Both full-fledged, full-time state certified health inspectors on our staff considered it a great degradation to have to enforce the outdoor code violations. It seemed especially beneath them to have to venture into the more unsavory parts of town and work. Traditionally, the new part-time guy is thrown headlong into the offensive locations to do battle with the riffraff and that's where I spent most of my time.

I would naively drive my shiny, unmarked police cruiser into some broken-down neighborhood, stop in front of a dilapidated house and begin filling out a complaint form. The card or crap game being played in the carport or garage would break up with half the players hightailing out the back and over fences while the remainder of the group would appoint someone to stroll out and see what I was up to. On more than one occasion I was approached by undercover cops who would instruct me to get the heck out of there because I was mucking up their drug sting. For this I left Colorado!

I quickly learned to vastly broaden my definition of junk and refuse. A twenty-year old car on blocks with weeds growing out of the hood in the back yard was not an inoperative vehicle; it was an antique that was lovingly being restored. A faded couch with three legs and torn upholstery on the front porch was serviceable lawn furniture. One man's trash as treasure almost always became my personal headache.

I once had a man arrested for not mowing his lawn. That may sound severe, but not to the neighbor who called it in because he could see the grass and weeds growing above the six-foot wooden fence that divided their back yards. When I went to check it out I could see the stuff growing over the fence from the street while seated in my car.

The home didn't seem inhabited so I decided to open the side gate to get a look at this jungle. Behind the gate stood the biggest, mangiest, meanest looking mastiff I had ever encountered or hope to again. That dog had tunneled pathways through the undergrowth and seemed most unhappy with his current situation. Fortunately, his shock at confronting me was just as great as mine to see him. In a panic I slammed the gate closed and ran for the safety of my cruiser. This provided great amusement for the watching neighbors.

The owner of this back yard run amok paid no heed to my letters and phone calls urging him to cut his grass. When he signed for my third and certified letter I wrote him a citation for ignoring me, which he also disregarded. Ignoring me was one thing, but ignoring the court got him arrested, jailed, fined and he still had to cut his grass.

When September rolled around one of the full-time health inspectors quit, which left an opening. My part-time job was over, but Rex, who I referred to as The Chief, liked my work and offered me the permanent position. I had enough science credits on my BA to qualify for certification and my six months on the job would count toward the state required one-year training period. All I had to do was take six weeks of classes, pass the state exam and the next thing you know I'm a Registered Health Inspector with the State of Texas.

The Holy Grail of a real job had yet to materialize and here was an offer that would pay the bills and provide full health care benefits. I'd become accustomed to telling the citizenry of Bliss to clean up their acts, so I signed on knowing I could keep searching for a career opportunity. I stayed with the City of Bliss for ten years, seven with the Health Department and three as the only Assistant Fire Marshal they'd ever had.

*I don't care who you think you are; don't mess with football
traditions in north Texas*

CHAPTER 3
FRIDAY NIGHT KINGS

Friday nights during the season in Texas are dedicated to high school football. This is true throughout most of the United States, but the fever burns most fervently in north Texas and Bliss was no exception. The men and boys that participate in the games are the kings of Friday nights. A good high school football coach is revered in his community and a winning record puts his prestige over the top.

Students and parents alike adore gifted football players. Failing grades can be repaired or overlooked for promising athletes, much to the dismay of the brainier bunch in the student body. Cheerleaders, booster club members, coaches, trainers and anyone else associated with the football program gain immediate status elevation.

Bliss High School was the home of The Brawling Backwoodsmen in spite of the fact that Bliss had not been a heavily wooded, uncultivated, thinly settled area since the school existed. Outside of Bliss the team was referred to as "The Bumpkins."

Concerted communal drives had been mounted several times over the years to change the team's name and update its image, but The Brawling Backwoodsmen were football tradition and nobody messes with football tradition in Bliss, Texas.

Slicing through the center of Bliss was a major U.S. Interstate which was the vital artery for traffic flow to all the tiny towns rapidly expanding on their own from the continued migration of adventurous commuters spending more and more of their day on the road between their country homes and jobs in Dallas. At the Main Street overpass stood a Bliss water tower in full view of the thousands of daily drivers passing through town. Emblazoned on the tower's mushroom-like reservoir was a giant depiction of a strapping Backwoodsman with the dates of seasons that the football team had won state championships. Occasionally the Backwoodsman's appearance would be altered to make him look more in tune with the current expectations of how a fine physical specimen should appear.

Every couple of years some merry prankster would scale the tower and endow the burly Backwoodsman with a monster Johnson. An immediate backlash of indignation would ricochet through the conservative sector of this Bible belt stronghold and the demand to quickly neuter the image would be swift and incessant. Meanwhile the actual Backwoodsmen players would swagger about as if they had newly awakened with astronomical appendages until the exaggeration was erased.

The football stadium at Bliss High School had been renovated over the years several times to keep it state of the art. Nothing was too good for the town's gridiron gladiators. The cost to keep pace with modern football technology was augmented by the booster club, which consisted of parents of current players, former players and local businesses that knew if they wanted to survive in Bliss donations were expected.

At Friday night home games the ample arena filled with local residents to capacity. Many of the men in jeans and cowboy boots limped from injuries sustained during their own glory days as Backwoodsmen. The game's outcome and quality of play would be a constantly recurring topic for the entire week to come until it was replaced by the next week's contest.

While performing a routine inspection in the Bliss High School cafeteria, I was approached by a slightly built young man wearing disturbingly thick glasses who was obviously not enamored by the school's football team. He appeared a little nervous, but strove to maintain a casual air about our interaction as hungry teenagers sauntered by with trays of bland, mass-produced food in segmented plates.

I was jotting notes on the inspection form attached to my clipboard when the lad sidled up next to me and said, "Please keep writing, but I want to ask you some questions."

I had not anticipated a clandestine meeting in this setting, but the urgency in his voice tweaked my curiosity so I kept my head down, continued writing and said, "Go ahead."

My informer looked around the room aimlessly and innocently and asked, "Do you guys inspect every place in Bliss that sells food?"

I wasn't sure if it was a trap or a trick, but I replied, "Sure. The state says we have to."

I think he giggled under his breath, but he managed to ask, "Then why don't you ever inspect the snack stands at the football stadium? You should see what they do in there; it's totally gross."

He slowly walked away without waiting for his answer and as I had suspected this was a trap. I was certain that the small snack stands in the stadium had never had a formal health inspection and I was sure without ever seeing them that they would not pass. Those stands raked in a ton of dough for the football team, and messing with that kind of moneymaker was going to cause me major migraines.

I finished up my cafeteria inspection and as usual the lunch ladies had done an impeccable job. I did have a question for the head lunch lady about finding what looked like mop strings in the holes of their massive dishwasher spray arms. That's exactly what they turned out to be. In their exuberance for creating the cleanest of conditions the last things to run through their industrial dishwasher at the end of the day were their mop heads. Even fastidious lunch ladies need a little oversight and the mop heads were relegated to overnight stays in a sanitizing solution in the mop sink.

I considered saying nothing of the encounter with the tattletale kid at the school when I returned to my office, but having a penchant for ruffling feathers kept me from keeping my mouth closed on this issue. Health Inspectors spend every day on their jobs telling people to do things they don't want to do, so how hard could this be?

I took a few deep breaths and thrust myself into the fog of the Chief's office. He must have been away for most of the day because I could easily make him out behind his desk in the haze. He looked up at me and I said, "Chief, we may have a tiny problem on our hands."

Rex did not like waves or wave makers. He told me the secret to his survival as a lifetime city employee was to stay low and out of the spotlight and try not to tick too many people off. He closed his eyes, rubbed his temples and said, "What now?"

Oh, man, Rex was already well into his daily sinus headache. I said, "It has been brought to my attention that we don't do inspections on the snack stands at the high school football field."

Poor Rex never opened his eyes when he replied, "What fool brought that up?"

I had not really thought much about how to dance around that question so I plowed ahead with, "Does it really matter? You know if somebody figured it out that sooner or later it's going to come up in some staff meeting and since our new city manager is so big on being proactive maybe we ought to go ahead and run with this thing." Not bad for getting caught flatfooted.

Rex lit a cigarette and there was still most of one burning in his ashtray. Slowly his eyes rolled open and it occurred to me that he looked like a catfish. He wiped away any hope of a smirk from my little epiphany by saying, "Fine. You deal with it, but I don't want to take any heat for this and I sure don't want it to cause me any trouble at the top. You got that?"

I got it, but I was pretty sure that there was no way to keep a lid on the outcome of this mission. I was about to mess with the money that supported football tradition.

I made a call to the high school principal, which put me in touch with the booster club president, who gave me a list of supporting parents and clubs that ran the snack bars at the football stadium. I set up meetings with people who had keys to their perspective stands for Monday figuring that any problems we might have could surely be worked out before Friday night's game.

Monday morning at stand number one I met Bill Westman. I recognized Bill as the owner of the used car lot on the east side of town. Bill gave me a big handshake and said, "You probably know my boy, John. He plays left tackle."

I didn't know anything about the Backwoodsmen's team, but Bill was pride swollen so I said, "Yeah, he's having a fine year."

Bill unlocked the door to the simple wooden hut and I stepped inside. It was just a wooden shell with a wooden counter and a sliding screen to hand food to customers. Oh no. I took out my state supplied standard inspection form and began to write. There was no required hand washing sink, no heat source for the food, no cleanable surfaces and so the list went on and on with check marks in the violations column.

Bill looked worried and I asked, "What do you serve from in here?"

Bill's face lit up and he said, "My wife makes the best tamales in the state. We always sell everything she can bring. It makes my whole house smell delicious on Fridays."

Yipes! Not only was this shed nowhere near being up to code, but the food was also coming from an unapproved and uninspected kitchen facility. I had to use a blank sheet to finish writing all the violations.

I went over my comments and concerns with Bill. He was stone quiet and his face grew more ashen by the minute. When I handed him the forms to sign he looked me right in the eye and said, "We can't do all this crap and still make money for the team. This stuff would cost a fortune. Don't you understand? We don't make a profit; we do this for the players."

I said, "Mr. Westman, I'm only going by the Health Code

requirements here. I'm not making any of this stuff up."

A little vein on Bill's forehead began to peak out from under his cowboy hat and his voice was very strained when he said, "Don't you remember what it was like when you played football?"

I should have thought before I answered, "I didn't play football in high school. I was on the baseball team."

Bill could not have recoiled in horror any faster if I had just informed him that I had herpes or leprosy. He stormed out of the shack with my carefully penned inspection forms crumpled in his fist and headed for the parking lot. I closed up the snack bar, put the padlock back on the hasp and went on to the next vender.

It was pretty much the same scenario with the remaining boosters. I could have copied Bill's violations and handed them out to the whole group. Instead of charging off in a full lather like Bill had done, the remaining stand operators were huddled up going over each other's reports when I headed back to the Health Department.

Rex was waiting outside the back door when I drove into the parking lot. Cigarette butts had been crushed all around his feet. He walked toward me as I got out of my vehicle and pointed across the lot at the city manager's office.

He greeted me with, "What have you done? My phone has run me out of my office and Dick wants to see us."

I grabbed my briefcase and said, "Is this about the snack stands?"

I thought Rex was going to go apoplectic on me. He shook with the words, "You better hope you can explain what you did today."

With that we marched into City Hall and straight to the City Manager's office. I had never met the man and had only seen him drive by a few times, but today he would be well aware of Ross Ryan and I was about to get a lesson in code interpretation. It would turn out to be one of the most important lessons of my ten-year career of enforcing codes and ordinances. You see no rule in this world is black and white. Special circumstances must be applied to all decisions regarding enforcement of regulations. The goal was not to simply go by the letter of the law, but always remember it's the intent of the law that matters. Intent would be the key ingredient in all my future decisions enforcing codes.

Mr. Dick Darling never offered me a seat when I entered his office. He was adding ashes to an already full ashtray when we came in and Rex joined him by lighting up. He spoke in measured tones and squinted just a tad when he said to me, "Are you the one causing me all this trouble today?" I nodded yes, but did not speak.

Dick went on, "I don't want to hear from another council member, school board official, alumni or business owner about those snack bars. Is that clear?"

I nodded my head again and said, "Yes, sir."

Dick added, "You figure out what we can do to make everybody happy and still meet the intent of the Health Codes. I'm sure there are some exceptions to be made in this case." I nodded to indicate I agreed and he waved us out of his presence.

Rex had a meeting of the minds back at the Health Department and we came up with some creative ways to get hands washed at the stands, keep the food at the proper temperatures and the good old lunch ladies pitched in by offering the school's kitchen for all the food preparations and storage of supplies.

I called a very long list of people to explain what was happening and went back to meet with all the snack shop operators with my hat in my hand. We did some simple renovations to make the floors and counter tops cleaning friendly and even Bill Westman shook my hand when it was all over. I don't care who you think you are; don't mess with football traditions in north Texas.

...his filth and slothfulness would not be tolerated in the city of Bliss!

CHAPTER 4

YES, YOUR HONOR

Not a lot of training was involved when I began working for Bliss. My friend, Bruce and I made a few sweeps around the city with him pointing out violations and me noting the specifics and exact locations of infractions to be inserted in form letters and mailed to property owners. It was usually better not to leave the car and venture forth onto some owner's land, so we carried a pair of binoculars to check for expired license plates and registration stickers from the street and to zoom in on debris to be itemized for removal.

A trip to City Hall would be needed to pour over public records in the tax and water department to pin down exactly who owned a parcel that needed to be brought up to code. Once the owner was documented a description of his dead car, detritus and overgrowth would be inserted into the blanks of the corresponding form letter by Pam and mailed off with a week or two given, depending on the size of the project, to right their wrongs. It was very common for property owners to hit the trifecta of code violations and receive a grass and weeds violation, inoperative vehicle and unsightly material notification in the same mailing.

Once a homeowner had been implicated as a violator, he would almost always lapse into a fit of finger pointing at his neighbors' transgressions. After the first domino had been tipped, a wave of reports would come flooding into my office and the entire neighborhood would be thrown into clean-up mode. I resented all the squealing on thy neighbors in the beginning, but learned to accept it as these people were doing my job--locating problems and bringing them to my attention with little or no effort on my part and then hounding each other until their whole little enclave would be shipshape.

In my rookie year I took great delight in composing letters individually tailored for exceedingly blatant violators. With thesaurus in hand I made every effort to make the recipients feel as though I had taken a personal interest in their case. Even these pointed diatribes would not always move the readers to action, and I would have to fall back on sending the certified generic threat with a citation zinger follow-up. Stubborn offenders would inevitably let the sequence play out to its legal conclusion by disregarding my citation, and a warrant for their arrest would automatically be issued. Being handcuffed on the job and dragged away to jail for having a ten-year-old pile of boards they considered to be a future shed by the side of their house would often move them to set a court date and force a showdown on the issue.

When the violator turned defendant appears in court, the health inspector who issued the citation and the city's attorney will be there to greet them. A well-prepared health inspector will have color photographs vividly illustrating the unwholesomeness of the blight to refute the glowing description the owner of the mess will inevitably present. The presiding judge will have the file depicting the chain of events that have caused us all to gather in court including copies of letters, dates of phone calls, pictures and any other communications that may have transpired.

A mere month into my tenured health inspecting career I found myself in court facing a persistent trash accumulating citizen that I just could not sway to clean up his act.

I watched as the judge perused one of my carefully crafted notices while the defendant droned on about the overall worth of a rotting pile of lumber and debris in his back yard. The judge's look of grave concern slowly faded to one of slight amusement as he realized the defendant was not going to mention the letter's contents and we were easily going to win this case. The judge looked up at me from the bench, pointed at my letter and mouthed the words, "You wrote this?" Indeed I had and shook my head in agreement.

Immediately following the hefty fine he imposed on my garbage gathering violator, the judge called a short recess and hauled me and the city attorney into a small adjoining room for a brief chat. "Do you read the letters these people send," the judge asked my attorney?

With a scowl on his face the attorney replied, "Well no, your honor."

The judge thrust my letter into the lawyer's hands and instructed, "By all means read this one!"

The attorney poured over my handiwork and stifled a grin when he came to the part where I had informed our newly convicted transgressor that, "…his filth and slothfulness would not be tolerated in the city of Bliss!" Evidently my blunt statement had jarred open some legal door for a libel suit, though the facts of the accusations were pretty plain to me. From that time on I was compelled to use only form letters, which were read by the Chief prior to Pam mailing them.

Occasionally I found myself defending some judgment call or decision I had made in the field and long forgotten. I responded to a complaint from a proprietor at a strip center store that sold health food and vitamins to investigate an odor that permeated the shop and made the owner and her employees nauseous. This unpleasant phenomenon occurred when the pet supply and grooming outfit in the next store would wash and dip dogs.

The health food store's owner was one of those thin, pasty looking gals who greeted me with a venomous sneer as soon as I walked in her door. She immediately began to assail me with a litany of physical woes she'd suffered from inhaling the noxious vapors that emanated from the pet shop. She was one unhappy camper.

It is always wise to seek the other side of any accusation so I went next door to chat with the pet shop folks. The owner was very cooperative, most apologetic and with nothing good to say had no comment regarding the health food lady. He had been lambasted by her daily regarding his release of alleged poisonous gases and was eager to resolve the problem.

I started my investigation by checking the label of pet shampoo/dip they were using. There were no dire health warnings in the manufacturer's fine print and we carried on with the probe.

Next I interviewed the workers who spent hours each day up to their elbows in the stuff and not one had suffered any ill effects. None of the owners had submitted any complaints or reservations after reclaiming their animals, which had been saturated with the offending substance and no customers who had entered the shop during the dog-dippings reported any problems. Last but not least, not one single pet whined or seemed to act adversely to being immersed in the maligned mixture and that's how I worded my report.

I did discover that the owner of the strip mall had saved a few coins by not extending the dividing wall between the two feuding shops all the way to the roof when he carved up the space to make two stores. The common air space above the drop ceilings allowed the rich aroma of pet shampoo to waft next door unimpeded. Being a drama queen prevented the health food storeowner from caring about this revelation. She looked me square in the eye and said, "By god, those people are slowly poisoning me and they're going to pay! You obviously don't know what you're doing. Get out of my store and don't come back."

I did have to go back to perform her routine health inspections, but she always hid in the back while I was there and had an assistant sign my report. There was an ugly incident regarding some bootleg goat's milk being sold from her place, but I never proved anything and hoped that my dealings with the wan one had ended.

It was four full years later that I was called to give a deposition in a room with no less than six attorneys regarding my findings at the pet shop. The case had finally come to court. I regretted my crack about the pets not complaining, but stuck to my guns regarding the lack of toxicity in the shampoo's vapor. Our little round table discourse was not friendly and I was thankful for the records I'd filed.

Bulging Eyes attorney asked me, "Mr. Ryan, what

qualifications and training do you have that make you an authority in this matter?"

I replied, "I am a licensed Health Inspector with the State of Texas."

Sharp Suit attorney counters with, "Do you have any formal instruction in the detection of dangerous odors and gasses."

I shot back, "Nope!"

Bulging Eyes smelled blood and hit me with, "What makes you think that you are capable of deciding that the dog shampoo in question was not toxic?"

I checked my notes and flippantly retorted, "I could not find any written indication that the vapors from that product could cause inhalers to suffer and other than the complainant, I could not find a single beast or human who had a problem with the stuff. I fell back on a big dose of common sense to draw my conclusions."

With that said the city's newly hired female attorney, Sheila Swift, called for a short recess and performed the equivalent of pulling me out of that meeting room by the ear. In her adjacent office Sheila scolded me, "You will not add anything to your answers. Make your replies simple, direct and void of personal feelings. You got that?" Boy, did I ever.

We went back into the meeting and the rest of the show consisted mostly of yes and no answers on my part. Even the health shop lady did not get a rise out of me when she said, "You didn't do your job correctly back then and you're still incompetent." I asked the stenographer if she got that accusation and Sheila gave me the hairy-eyeball, but we managed to finish up the proceedings without any more private tutoring.

There was no mistaking the fact the health food lady still

hated me and I was never called to court. Her attorneys must not have viewed my testimony as a plus for her case. A friend who served on the ensuing trial's jury called to tell me the judge ruled against the health food lady. I could muster no surprise or compassion for the verdict.

Denise, it's only the ghosts; go back to sleep.

CHAPTER 5
HOW DID I END UP HERE?

It's one thing to move out of state to be a ski-bum for four years after leaving home for four years to attend college, but moving back in with your parents with eight years of living single under your belt is not a recipe for a harmonious domestic environment. It's not that Jack and Donna Ryan were ready to kick their oldest son out on the streets, but having him reoccupy his old room was a situation they had not anticipated.

To complicate matters further one of my older sisters had returned to the nest with a husband and two preschool age children while they constructed a cabin in the country. My poor father who had seen all but one of his kids grow up and move out of his house was now faced with them returning and dragging along offspring of their own. I had to get out of there fast.

In my last year of college I lived in an attic room with a friend from high school days. His father had the foresight to help him into a house where he could rent rooms to his buddies while we all attended the same north Texas university. Bart Pollex still lived in that house and was still renting rooms. It was not a massive stride forward, but I was one step ahead of my boyhood bedroom when I moved back into Bart's place.

An instant added bonus to living north of Bliss meant the daily commute to work was suddenly much easier. It would be many years in the future before traffic between Demon and Bliss would attain the same ugly congestion as the clogged driving arteries of the immediate Dallas area.

An additional boon was the availability of beer. Texas is a funny place when it comes to drinking regulations and the invention of 'dry-counties', 'dry-cities' or even 'dry- areas' within a city is a Bible belt phenomenon that never made any sense to me. Bliss was dry. You could not purchase any form of consumable alcohol in Bliss, but the adjacent town of Hollyhock Hill would be glad to sell you all you wanted and reap the rewards of tax dollars and profits in the process.

There were no beer stores between Bliss and my folk's house in a suburb west of Dallas. When I was growing up people had to drive into Dallas to buy spirits or to consume them in a bar, club or restaurant. It was called "crossing the river" because the Trinity River was the dividing line between our dry suburb and wet Dallas.

Forbidding people from buying alcohol in my hometown did nothing to deter anyone that wanted to drink from doing so; it just meant they would have to drive back across the Trinity liquored-up to get home instead of drinking at home where it was safer. Many beer runs or nights on the town ended with a crash on the long bridges spanning the Trinity River or on the well-worn back roads that lead to legal liquor stores.

North of Bliss I could buy beer on my way home, which was often comforting after being yelled at all day by taxpayers who felt they were entitled to verbally abuse a public official. Demon was damp, which meant they could sell beer and wine, but not hard liquor. This concession to the college age drinkers in town had come after many failed campaigns to get the good churchgoers to legalize adult beverages. People still had to drive to buy liquor or drink it in a watering hole or restaurant, which put them back on the roads happily impaired. It's all very confusing and will always remain that way.

On my meager part-time salary I could live comfortably at Bart's. There was a second renter in one of the two downstairs rooms to help cover the cost of shared utilities. Having three bachelors in the place did not always make for the tidiest of environments, but there was always someone to grouse with about work, watch sporting events or join for carousing about town.

After my summer stint the salary increase that came with obtaining full-time health inspector status allowed me to move into a place all my own. I lucked into a modern duplex that had been vacant for months. I could not have afforded all the rent myself, but the owner was desperate for some income so she let me have it for half the normal rent with the proviso that I would allow a roommate to move in if she could find one that we both deemed acceptable.

I had barely settled into my fortunate situation when I discovered the place was haunted. I kept a small nightlight burning in the living area of my digs and awoke in the middle of the night to see shadowy figures walking around my dining room table. I immediately sought the protection afforded by hiding under my covers and didn't peak out again until my involuntary shivering abated. By that time the shadows were gone.

I got out of bed and turned on every light in every room of the house and looked into every corner and closet for a logical explanation for my sighting. I found nothing. I checked to make sure all the drapes were tightly closed and no light could get through from the outside to dance around the room and cause apparitions. The place was sealed up tight. There were no drafts and no explanations for what I'd seen.

A few weeks went by and I never breathed a word about my ghosts to a soul for fear of being branded a lunatic. I didn't really believe in ghosts and had mostly forgotten about them when I awoke in the wee hours one morning to find the shadows cavorting around my living room once again.

This time I bolted out of bed and switched on the lights. There was nothing there. I went through the total house search routine again and came up clueless.

My silent ghosts returned on many nights after those first sightings. They never made noise, never moved anything and never bothered me. I can't explain why I would wake to see them shuffling around my living room when they were so darn considerate and quiet. I found the courage to call out to them on a few occasions, but they never acted like they heard me and kept milling around unless I got out of bed, which caused them to vanish.

One night my girlfriend stayed over and I was awakened by tiny, rapid kicks, like a nervous rabbit might make, to my right leg. She was wide-eyed and pointing into the living room when I rolled over to see why I'd been rudely aroused. I looked through the doorway to discover that she had espied my specters.

I lay back down and calmly said, "Denise, it's only the

ghosts; go back to sleep."

Denise whispered, "What do you mean, it's only the ghosts?"

I wearily answered, "They're here all the time. Trust me they won't bother you; now please go back to sleep."

Denise didn't sleep much the rest of that night, but the ghosts didn't bother her either. I was happy that someone else had seen them and we would both encounter their wispy forms on future nights.

My original six-month lease came and went with no roommate. I agreed to go on a month-by-month extension and four more months slipped by. Then my landlady announced that she'd given up and sold the place. The new owners planned to live there and I would have to vacate in thirty days. I wondered if she knew about the ghosts, but I didn't want to ask for fear of sounding unbalanced.

I found a slightly run-down house in one of the older neighborhoods of Bliss and moved. My ancient landlord was an old school bubba and after we agreed on a deposit and a monthly rent amount, the deal was sealed with a handshake. The house was small and harbored a lively bug population, but I had it all to myself and it was only blocks away from the Health Department in Old Town.

Six weeks rolled by and there was a knock at my door around dinnertime one evening. It was my aged landlord with sad news to go with the big sad eyes with which he greeted me. He had come to tell me that his children were taking control of his assets and they had sold my house in the process. I would have to vacate the place in two weeks.

I was in no way prepared for this revelation and asked,

"Can't I talk with the new owners? Maybe they'll rent the place to me?"

My subdued landlord shook his head and replied, "No, the new owners plan to move into this house. They are a Mexican family with six kids and I'm pretty sure they aren't going to try and make room for you." He shuffled off to his truck and slowly drove away.

I was more than a tad panicky. With no written lease I knew I had to be packed up and gone in fourteen days. There had not been many places available in my price range when I found this one, and Bart was renting my room to a new attic dweller in Demon.

I went into urgent search mode for a new abode. In all of Bliss I could not find a single listing in the paper that I could afford. I had resorted to driving up and down residential streets in my quest of a place to live between checking on complaints at work. That's when I stumbled on a tiny garage apartment a block from my current house and even closer to my office.

I was cruising slowly down a very small lane looking for the address of a violator who was alleged to have been harboring four inoperative vehicles on his property. I located the small wrecking yard in the middle of the block and began to write down the dead vehicles' descriptions and license numbers.

I got the goods on my outlaw and drove on down the street. There at a ninety-degree bend in the end of the road were two women working from a small truck on a garage apartment barely visible from the road. I pulled into their drive and walked back to the open door of the tiny structure.

The two ladies who greeted me inside were domestic partners that owned several rental units scattered around Bliss.

One was wearing paint-splattered overalls and the other had on a business dress and heels. They were arguing about the color being applied to the kitchen cabinets but stopped in mid fight to see what I wanted.

I said, "Good day, ladies. Is this place for rent?"

Heels answered, "It will be in a few days if we can get it fixed up by then."

Overalls chimed in, "Don't worry, I'll be done when your ad comes out in the paper, that is if you'll leave me alone long enough to finish my work."

Heels turned on Overalls and said, "You're dragging this project out too long. I've already paid for that ad and I need to be able to show this place to prospective renters."

Overalls lifted the brush in her hand and pointed it toward Heels and said, "I told you not to worry, now leave me alone and let me finish the job."

I cut in on their argument, "Excuse me, but I may be able to solve your problem."

They both stopped bickering and looked at me again. Heels asked, "Just how is that?"

I said, "I need a place to live in seven days. I'm currently living just around the corner from here, which would make the move easy and I work for the city at the Health Department two blocks away."

Overalls asked, "Why the sudden urge to move?"

I admitted, "I've had my place sold out from under me and I only had a verbal lease."

Both ladies laughed at my confession. Heels stopped first and said, "Well, you'll have to sign a real lease if you rent from us, and we'll need to check your background information."

I responded, "I have no problem with that."

Overalls wrinkled her brow and asked, "Don't you even want to look around the place?"

I laughed and shot back, "Unless some of it is underground I think I can see it all from here." That was a fact. The little two-car garage was one open room with a small kitchen area in the far corner. A tiny bedroom and bathroom had been added on the back. My king-size bed would fill the bedroom with just enough space to open the drawers of my dresser if I was not standing in front of them when they were pulled out.

Both ladies walked over and shook my hand. Heels said, "I'm Ruth and this is my partner, Beth. Welcome aboard, that is assuming you checkout OK."

I said, "Ladies, it's a pleasure to meet you. I'll be a good renter."

Beth warned me that, "I won't be done here for a couple more days, but you can move in after that."

Ruth knitted her brow, gave me the once-over and asked, "You do realize where you are don't you? I mean we always have a devil of a time renting this place because of the street's name."

I shook my head and confessed that, "Yes, I'm painfully aware of the street's name and feel as though I'm about to pay some dues for all the times I've made fun of it. I would never have dreamed that I would have this street name for an address, but I'm desperate and if the price is right I can handle the teasing."

Ruth shot me a rent amount that was almost half of what I'd been paying and I agreed to a six-month lease. That is how I ended up living on Fagg Drive and renting a miniscule garage apartment from two of the nicest lesbian landlords anyone could ever hope to do business with in this life. I stayed at the Fagg Drive address for five years. It was just too cheap to give up and I loathe moving.

Living on Fagg Drive compelled me to do some research into how the tiny street got its name. One of the founding fathers and a former mayor of Bliss had been born a Fagg long before the family name carried today's stigma. There were very few people outside of Bliss and not many Bliss residents who knew the history behind the street's moniker.

Divulging that I lived on Fagg Drive would always draw laughter or scorn, but never a neutral response. The amount of times I had to repeat my address when I moved to this new location was astounding and time consuming when I had to weather the inevitable over-reactions. There were forms to fill out for the bank, utilities, work and credit card companies. I didn't delude myself into thinking that all my friends and family members were going to let an opportunity to lampoon me for living on Fagg slip by unheralded, and they didn't disappoint.

I resorted to spelling Fagg instead of pronouncing it when giving a verbal account of my new location. My favorite conversation regarding my unusual address occurred while renewing my Playboy subscription. I called the magazine's delivery department to report my change of locale and was put on the line with one of those gals that cooed in a smooth voice that sounded as if she had just swallowed a quart of cocoa butter. Her phone nom de plume was Heather.

Heather breathlessly answered my call, "Hello, this is Playboy. What can I do to make your day better?"

She sounded so intimate and I answered, "I moved and need

to change the address on my magazine subscription."

Heather oozed back, "Well we wouldn't want you to miss a single issue, now would we?"

I feigned concern saying, "Heavens no! I'd get so far behind on my reading. Some days those articles are all that keep me going."

Laughingly Heather asked, "What is the name and new address for your subscription?"

I gave her my name and the street number and then spelled out, "F-A-G-G Drive."

There was a short pause while she typed and then a slight snicker. Another pause and then Heather came back on the line. Trying not to laugh she repeated, "F-A-G-G?"

I said, "Yup!"

There was a long pause and then Heather broke into uncontrollable laughter. Heather's laughter sounded pretty and wasn't insulting. It was genuine laughter from amusement. She had me chuckling when she finally composed herself and came back on the line to apologize. "Mr. Ryan, you have got to be kidding me! I've been doing this for years and there has never been a Playboy subscriber living on Fagg Drive that I know of."

I said, "No, that's it. Chalk me up as your first Fagg resident."

Heather stifled another round of laughter and choked out, "We have got to find you a new place to live. I mean really."

I did eventually move to the west side of town, but not until City Hall changed locations and not to make Heather happy. I just hope that back in his day Mr. Fagg did not have to fight his way to school and back because of his family's name.

I put the seven pages of heinous violations from the kitchen in my briefcase and got a clean page to work on before mingling with the diners so as not to overly alarm anyone.

CHAPTER 6
EGGS & MORE

The Bliss Health Department used an archaic but functional accounting method to keep track of routine health inspections for its rapidly growing number of food service establishments. Every location in town that prepared food had its own three- by five-inch note card. The cards were split in two even groups and kept in plastic boxes. When I started we performed monthly inspections. Bruce took one box, I took the other and we would trade them off at the end of the month with the date that we visited each site neatly noted on its card.

The inspector who vacated my position had been carefully penning his inspection dates on these tiny cards for years without ever actually visiting any of the businesses. Before I came along the boxes were not traded and the same inspector performed his duties at the same locations purportedly building a strong relationship with the proprietors and seeing through all the needed repairs and improvements that were discovered. Business owners never complained about the lack of scrutiny, and reports were filed without signatures or added notations, just happy little checkmarks in all the right places to show that all was well in the bistros of Bliss.

Bruce knew about the lack of oversight regarding the listings in the hand-me-down card box and elected to give it to me when our corrupt compeer bolted from the department. He never said anything about the constant omissions as they did not reflect directly on him and nobody was raising any objections to the process.

Ms. Beaula was gone by the time I graduated from just enforcing outdoor code violations to inspecting restaurants and the new city honcho, Dick Darling, tossed an added challenge into the works when I headed off to confront the food processors in my acquired box. Bliss was blossoming and more money was going to be needed to expand the city's work force and keep tabs on the progress. To avoid the ungainly political ramifications of raising taxes to add to the city coffers, we would institute permit fees for performing the same tasks city employees had always done. The idea behind selling this strategy was to place the burden of costs more directly on the users and not spread it among the entire populace.

To save time and money inspectors would introduce shopkeepers to the new fee structure during their regular visits. Owners who already adored health inspectors for pointing out costly needed repairs and filthy conditions that required immediate attention would naturally be overjoyed by the news of this added financial onus and embrace the idea with great gusto.

I carefully selected the first restaurant from my benign looking Pandora's box on the merits of its past inspections and popularity with city department heads and employees. Every bigwig in Bliss frequented the Eggs & More eatery. County officials, state and local lawmen and area business leaders also made it a point to swing by before the day's doings got under way to keep in touch with the people that made things happen. With all these power brokers frequenting the restaurant and the stack of glowing previous reports surely this would be the perfect location to ease into my new role.

With my Health Inspector's cap squarely in place, I parked behind the crumbling strip center where the Eggs & More was located and followed the trail of crusting food orts that led from the reeking dumpsters to the back door. The torn screen had been thrown aside and the battered metal door was ajar. I let myself into the kitchen during the breakfast rush and lurched into the grimy trashcans that were serving as bulk food bins when I slid across the greasy floor.

As I regained my footing on the slippery tiles a grizzly man in a gravy stained apron with a stump of a cigar in the corner of his jaw came across the room to confront me. He was the owner, Rance Smith, and he did not look easily approachable. Rance spat out at me above the din, "Just who do you think you are, and what in tarnation are you doing in my kitchen?"

I stood tall and wiped some goop off my briefcase before replying, "My name is Ross Ryan, and I'm a health inspector with the city of Bliss. I'm here to do your routine inspection."

Rance took a step back and scratched a blotch on the side of his balding pate. He shifted the stump of cigar to the other side of his mouth and said, "Health inspector? I didn't even know Bliss had a Health Department. When did all this come about?"

Employees continued to scurry around us as if we did not

exist, and I raised my voice to clear the sound of crashing tableware and hissing steamers, "I've got copies of all your past inspections in here." I pointed at my new briefcase with the fresh stain on its fake leather exterior.

Rance knitted his brows, threw up his hands and shouted, "Well, it's the first I've ever heard of it and I've been here a long time. I've got a breakfast crowd out there and more to do than you can believe. Can't you come back some other time?"

A smarter man would have jumped at this free escape offer, but I still didn't have a clear picture of what I'd gotten myself into. I shook my head no and told Rance, "You just go about your business and I'll do my job. We'll talk about it when I'm done."

Rance turned and went back to cooking on an ancient range under a vent hood that was dripping grease into a coffee can on the corner of the cooking surface. I pulled out a pen and my forms and went to work.

Rex had seen to it that we now used the latest health inspection forms recommended by the State of Texas. These new self-copying forms not only required an owner's signature and date at the bottom, but also included blank pages to list infractions that weren't explained by simply checking boxes in the neat categories listed on the formal document. Required items now carried a number value that added up to 100 when everything was copasetic. The resulting scores would indicate how clean a given restaurant operated and could be listed for comparison in the local paper.

Some towns had a set low score that would require the inspector to close the establishment. Rex wanted no part of any arbitrary number causing a business to be locked down and instructed us to never close a place unless an imminent health hazard existed.

I was about to find out exactly what that meant.

I glanced around the room and marveled at the chaos that is the norm for any commercial kitchen during their peak meal serving hours. What was not normal was the appalling filth and run-down state of this kitchen. I didn't bother with the regular report forms and placed a stack of blank sheets on my clipboard.

I decided to start by the back door and work my way slowly around the kitchen noting each infraction in detail along the way. I had filled an entire page with single-spaced and neatly printed notes before I got out of the back entry hall. I knew that there were going to be some in-depth explanations required on my part when this exercise was completed, and I was going to have the whole disgusting mess well documented.

When I finished the kitchen the breakfast crowd was long gone and the lunch crowd had begun to trickle in. By the time I got to the dining area the place was full again. I put the seven pages of heinous violations from the kitchen in my briefcase and got a clean page to work on before mingling with the diners so as not to overly alarm anyone. It was also filled completely before I left the salad and food bars that had been set-up for the noon buffet. The hot foods were not hot enough, the cold foods were not cold enough and nothing on, near, over or under the buffet tables was clean enough to pass muster.

Thank God the Eggs & More did not serve dinner. The kitchen staff was going through the half-hearted motions that comprised their cleanup procedures before closing when Rance found me in a booth finishing my report and asked, "How'd we do?"

All I could say was, "It's bad. It's real bad!"

Rance chuckled and said, "Aw now, it can't be as bad as all that. Let's see what you got there."

I handed him the last page I'd been working on. He was scanning over its lengthy lamentations when I dug out the seven remaining pages of grief.

Rance stopped reading, wiped his hands on the front of his already blackened apron and said, "You have got to be kidding me?"

I shook my head and told him, "It's all in there and none of it is good."

Lance tossed the papers on the booth's table and asked, "Son, how long you been doing this?"

I confessed, "This is my first real restaurant inspection since I got my Health Inspector's Certification and finished training, so I'm sure there's a lot of stuff I missed."

Lance pointed at the kitchen and said, "Well then, let's me and you just go in there and see what all this stuff you wrote down means."

We walked into the now empty kitchen and got started. By the back door the trashcans that held bulk flour and cornmeal were dirty, cracked and one had ants coming out a hole in the bottom while the other was supporting a burgeoning weevil colony. I pointed out the grease and grime on the walls, floor, doorknobs and ceiling in the area and explained that it just got worse the farther I went into the kitchen so I wouldn't bring it up at every stop.

We went into the walk-in cooler and I noted that the wooden skids that had been put down because the floor had rusted through were not cleanable and the food that had fallen between the slats and rotted was the cause of the nasty smell inside. The rusty racks of uncovered foods were broken and needed cleaning and the holding temperature inside the refrigerator unit had never gotten within 10 degrees of the required minimum the whole time I'd been there.

I stopped to open the door to the small closet that held the under-sized water heater on our way to the cooking areas. The light that flooded in set the thousands of cockroaches that had been feasting on the food and debris that was pushed under the door for probably years into a frantic search for darkness. I told Rance that the initial shock of all those bugs almost caused me to miss the rodent dropping near the back of the closet.

Standing in front of the dilapidated cooking ranges I explained that catching old grease that dripped from the vent hoods above in a coffee can was better than letting it splash on the griddle's cooking surfaces, but pulling down the filters and washing out the ducts was a far better solution. Everything in the kitchen was sorely in need of a thorough scrubbing and the rusted appliances and utensils would all have to be replaced.

Rance stopped me before I made it out of the kitchen's quagmire to point out that his buffet tables didn't maintain proper temperatures for holding food. He'd had enough and it was all starting to sound pretty redundant anyway.

I had him sign every page of my inspection and told him that I'd never even heard of a restaurant scoring a 32. I was positive that his establishment met the criteria of an imminent health hazard and that there was no way I could let him open again until the place was cleaned up and repairs made to the equipment that didn't have to be replaced.

Rance played his political card on me and asked with a slight smirk, "Do you realize who all eats in this joint? I mean your city manager was at that very table this morning, like just about every other morning and half the state troopers start their day at my place. You might ought to check with your boss before you go shutting me down?"

I was worn out, felt disgustingly dirty and did not hesitate to reply, "If I get nailed for closing this place in the shape it's in, then there's no use inspecting anywhere else."

Rex had stationed himself at his usual haunt among a pile of old butts by the back door of the jail when I drove into the parking lot. I knew Rance would have made as many calls for clemency as possible before I got back to the office. I got out of my car and headed for the City Manager's office without Rex even saying a word. He was hot on my heels in a cloud of smoke.

From the looks of him, Dick Darling's day had been no better than my own. He started in on me from his desk before I even got into his office. "Why is it always you that stirs up a stink that lands on me? Did you have to go after the one place in town that caters to every mover and shaker in north Texas? What can you possibly have to say for yourself?"

I looked at Rex for some support, but since all he knew about my inspection was what Rance had shouted at him over the phone, he took another drag from his cigarette and stared emotionless from that catfish face of his. I turned back to Dick and said, "I closed the Eggs & More because they had roaches, rodents, ants and rotten food." I pulled my thick dossier of inspection copies out of my dirty briefcase and handed them to Dick.

To my surprise Dick actually started perusing my documents. By the third page he looked up and asked, "My God, how long has this been going on and why hasn't something been done before now? This didn't just happen overnight."

It was apparent that Rex was going to let me hang myself on this one so I chimed right in, "It would seem that the previous inspector, who is no longer with the city, failed to bring these problems to the owner's attention. That inspector is long gone, but it still doesn't change what I saw and how bad the Eggs & More really is."

Dick had gone back to reading my forms while I was fumbling with an excuse and he looked up again around page five. "I'll send these over after I have copies made. It looks like we need to find a better place to drink our coffee in the morning. Get out."

I did not know my new boss well enough yet to kid with him as we traipsed across the parking lot to our little jail. He motioned for Bruce to leave his desk and join us in his office as we went down the short hallway from the back door.

Rex sat with somewhat of a thud behind his desk and I closed the door before sitting next to Bruce in front of him. He lit his next cigarette from the remnants of the one he'd been nursing in Dick's office and let us stew for a minute. With his cigarette dangling from his lower lip he crossed his hands on the blotter in front of him and slowly said, "If you get into a situation in the field that looks like it's going to ruin my day or possibly my career for the love of God call me. I don't want to hear it from Dick first. I don't want the person you're dealing with to call me first. I want it to come from your lips as soon as you think that there's going to be a stink. Got that?"

Bruce and I looked at each other, back at Rex and replied in unison, "Yes, sir."

I could tell that I'd really aged Rex with this stunt. Dick must have unloaded on him before I got back. I should have come straight to the office instead of checking on some code violations after the restaurant inspection. Rex closed his bulging eyes, rubbed his temples and was mumbling something about me causing his early death while we were walking out after he told us to leave.

Outside Bruce said, "You didn't really close the Eggs & More?"

I said, "Yup, you should have seen it in there. It was too gross for words."

Bruce was laughing when he replied, "Better you than me. You have got a lot to learn about working for a city. I predict a pretty short career if you keep this up."

The Eggs and More never re-opened. It was too far-gone to salvage. Rance Smith surfaced as the manager of a few other small eateries over the years, but he never owned another restaurant in Bliss. The local big dogs and bosses must have located a breakfast joint in another town to conduct morning pre-business chitchats. My first of many restaurant inspections had been a real doozey and put another blemish on my ever-deteriorating relationship with the City Manager.

*Here was this big strong guy with enough firepower in his
pants to down a bull elephant and he ran like a frightened
deer from a dog locked up in an orange Pinto.*

CHAPTER 7
JOCKO JOINS THE TEAM

City government is at the bottom of the pecking order when
the day's duties are doled out. The State of Texas decided that many
of the tasks that state inspectors were doing could best be handled
at the local level and notified Rex that they would no longer come
around and perform the required inspections at State Licensed
day-care centers, senior centers, mental health facilities, hospitals,
schools and the list went on, but the message was that we were on
our own to take care of these places. We would also need to forward
our findings to the state so they could continue to collect license
fees and issue operating papers. Since none of the owners, operators
or inspectors in Bliss could remember ever actually seeing a state
inspector perform his job it was going to be another introduction by
Bliss Health Inspectors to jubilant business owners regarding the
intricacies of state mandates.

With the success of rolling the state's work downhill the
County began to take a hard look at its Health Department. So much

of the unincorporated land in Demon County had been annexed into the ever-expanding towns and cities that the bulk of the County Health Department was deemed to be no longer needed.

The Demon County Health Department was run by a muscled-up bunch of near hooligans who had grown up in the area and spent most of their time in an old-style gym near the Demon town square pumping themselves up with free weights and consuming body mass-producing chemicals. With only the occasional septic system installation to occupy them they had long since fallen into the habit of easing into work late in the mornings, taking prolonged lunch breaks and utilizing the afternoon movie matinees to fill in the bulk of their business days. It was no surprise that their services were not missed when the ax fell sending their licensed inspectors scurrying for employment.

Rex viewed our newfound workload as added job security. The note cards began to bulge from our little inspection boxes, causing me and Bruce to resort to bi-monthly inspections and still we could not keep up with the explosive growth. Dick was pleased with all the new permits we would be issuing to establishments that now fell under our jurisdiction and therefore was amenable to the hiring of a third inspector to help us out.

Enter Jocko Marks. Jocko had power lifted enormous weights at a competitive level for many years, but he was fast reaching that point in life and his athletic career when he needed to accept the fact that he was no longer a wild kid. He was by far the saner of the two Marks brothers who had worked for the Demon County Health Department, but he was still prone to ingesting large quantities of dubious substances to enhance a vague notion that he would once again compete at the state level in his age group. Jocko was a nice guy and we were relieved that he was chosen over his more unstable peers, but he was subject to some pretty wacky mood swings when he was on the juice and it was usually best to approach him in a cautious manner.

Surprisingly, Jocko had a good work ethic, and he provided an immediate relief to the load that Bruce and I were staggering under when he hired on as inspector number three. The cards in our little file boxes were split three ways and we could once again close them.

Bruce and I maintained offices in the two rear cells of our miniscule hoosegow and Jocko moved into the coffee room. It was a larger area than our cells but shared a wall with Rex's smoke tank and was subject to the constant coming and going of people needing coffee or seeking the comfort of the building's lone toilet. Jocko didn't like smoke and he didn't drink coffee, but he sure gave that crapper a daily workout.

It takes a ton of food to fuel a power lifter, and I had witnessed Jocko eating an entire chicken plus fixin's by himself during one of the few lunch outings we shared. Jocko went at meals like performing a chore, with his fork sticking up from a clenched fist before he lowered his head and went about scooping and inhaling his food. There would be no conversation until the meal was completed, and it was like watching a vacuum cleaner with teeth work.

Jocko was so tight he squeaked when he walked. To save cash he resorted to bringing all his meals in paper sacks and consuming them in his truck. No matter how cold or swelteringly hot, Jocko would never run the truck's engine to condition the air as it wasted fuel and therefore money.

Normally Health Inspectors performed their duties in Lone Ranger fashion. Occasionally it was wise to take someone along as back-up or just to have another witness to some outlandish discovery made during the course of the day.

I had taken yet another anonymous complaint regarding the abandonment of vehicles and construction equipment in a less than savory portion of town and decided I could use some company checking it out. I would have to leave a remote blacktop alley and walk several hundred yards down a rutted dirt road into a weed-choked field to copy the serial numbers off the vehicles and equipment I'd spotted with my binoculars and asked Jocko to come along and cover my back.

We got out of my truck at the entrance to the sinister looking lots, and Jocko told me he had a bad feeling about the place. The questionable vehicles were bunched under the few trees near the back of the field and barely discernable in the late afternoon's shadows. We would have to hike down the muddy road through tons of discarded trash and debris to record their descriptions and hopefully vehicle identification numbers. It was still and very quiet.

Before we started Jocko said, "I think they're all stolen and the bad guys aren't too far away from here. It looks like some of that stuff gets used now and then, and then they hide it back here."

This was not a brilliant revelation but reasonable under the circumstances and I replied, "Good. If all that junk is hot then the police can deal with it and I won't have to come back out here."

Jocko raised his shirt to show me a very large pistol he'd tucked into the waist of his pants and said, "I thought we could use some insurance."

Now I really had the heebie-jeebies! Neither of us was licensed or authorized to be carrying a weapon around on the job, much less a cannon like the one Jocko flashed me. I shook my head and said, "Just don't shoot me with that hog leg or fool around and blow off your lower unit trying to quick draw that thing out of your pants. You're way too big for me to drag out of here if you go down."

Off we went with me on point picking our way around ruts full of stagnant water and garbage. When we got to the shade trees there were a couple of big trucks that could no doubt be used to pull the equipment stashed in the weeds around them. The strange thing was that this was all road-surfacing equipment with the State of Texas logos embossed on their sides.

I copied down the state's identification numbers from their yellow equipment, the truck's plates and started to leave. Jocko pointed out an orange Pinto that had no wheels and was just discernible under a camouflaging pile of weathered cardboard and whispered, "You might as well get the VIN number off that thing. We don't want to have to come back down here anytime soon."

I eased over to the driver's side of what was left of the car and peered through the cracked windshield in hopes that the vehicle's identification number tag would still be attached to the dashboard. It was there but rust made the tiny numerals hard to read. I started to open the driver's door to poke my head inside the car when hot slobber was slung through the top of the door's window that had been left rolled down about six inches. Appearing immediately behind the barrage of drool was the unmistakable shape of the monster pit bull's head whose nap I'd just interrupted. The pit bull unloaded a guttural roar and bit hard into the window's glass as it lunged with all its might into the Pinto's door.

It lunged again and I staggered backward and fell to one knee before completing my turn to run for it. My back-up was nowhere to be seen. Had I been between Jocko and my truck when he hightailed it for safety he would have trampled me to death. I heard a man's yell from beyond the weeds and trees where I knew a few decrepit houses lined the next block and I redoubled my escape efforts.

When I reached my truck Jocko had taken up a defensive position on its far side. Had I not locked my vehicle and taken the keys I'm sure my ride and Jocko would have been long gone when I arrived.

I wasted no time opening my door and starting up the little truck's engine. Jocko's door failed to unlock the first few times I released the mechanism because he was pulling frantically on the handle. I could see the silhouette of what I assumed to be an angry man lumbering toward us down the dirt road through Jocko's window. Jocko finally let go of the door's handle long enough for it to unlock so he could jump inside. We sped away.

Once I got onto a main thoroughfare I pulled over and looked Jocko right in the eye. "What happened to our insurance?"

Jocko's eyes were wide and wild when he replied, "Did you see the size of that beast?"

With a blank stare I said, "I got a pretty good look at it there from about two inches. What the heck happened to you?"

Jocko still looked shook up, but he explained, "I hate those things. They're killers. I worked with Animal Control at the County and I saw what those things could do. All I could think of was getting the heck out of there."

"So, thanks a lot, Jocko. What about me?"

Jocko shook his head and managed a little smile when he said, "Man, I'm sorry. I bailed on ya, but you gotta admit that was one scary SOB."

We both laughed about it on the way back to our teeny jail. Here was this big strong guy with enough firepower in his pants to down a bull elephant and he ran like a frightened deer from a dog locked up in an orange Pinto. Of course, I ran like a frightened girl, but I was within slobbering distance of the thing when it broke the day's silence. I learned not to count on Jocko when things got eerie, and he told me to call a cop next time I wanted to play hero in an area where people steal and stash State owned equipment.

The stolen equipment was recovered and it had been taken from a State project on the outskirts of town. The police whined about the warning we'd given the thieves which kept them from nabbing anyone for the crime, but I got my field cleaned up and closed the file on another complaint without getting my rear end chewed off so Rex was good with the outcome. We never mentioned Jocko's gun to anyone.

CHAPTER 8
WHY'S THE LAWN SO LUSH?

In most cities the Health Inspector's job covers a heck of a lot more than just surprising and exacerbating restaurant owners and managers. The smaller the town the broader the scope of duties will be for the Health Inspector. In Bliss this was covered at the end of every employee's job description. Right after the list of regularly assigned tasks was this mouthful: "…and perform all other miscellaneous duties as needed."

Having recently been more rural than citified Bliss would occasionally provide the Health Department with a loathsome example of a malfunctioning septic system. These discoveries would usually come about when the unmistakable aroma of human dispatches would surface to haunt some unsuspecting new development downwind of the perpetrator's lateral lines. A desperate call would come into the Health Department and an inspector would be sent to seek the source of the reek.

Once the bailiwick of the County Health Department septic systems within Bliss's city limits were now the city's problem.

Having dealt with such odious ordeals in unincorporated Demon County, Jocko was our septic system specialist, but he was quick to impart what he knew to the rest of us in order to avoid becoming the "Lone Excrement Expert."

The basic concept of designing a septic system could not be simpler. With no handy city sewer main to connect with, the collective discharges from a site are piped into an underground septic tank or tanks sized for the anticipated loads to be generated. The bulkier portion of the unwanted waste should remain in the tank to be dealt with microbiologically until, like the mostly moisture portion of the program, it travels up and into the lateral lines. Hopefully the liquid reaching the lateral lines will have left its foul odoriferousness in the tank. The remaining moisture is supposed to be soaked up by the ground and plants or evaporate into the air. The lateral lines are sized for the anticipated flow and the moisture absorbing qualities of the surrounding ground. The lines are laid perfectly level to evenly distribute the incoming tide. When it all works according to plan, it is truly a miraculous thing.

Human error, mechanical failure and the forces of nature all interact to exact a toll on the lowly septic system. The most common incidence of disappointment must be directly attributed to the designer grossly underestimating or never anticipating the amount of expected influx the system will have to handle. Classic examples include the man who moved into a house with six daughters, the young couple who suddenly found themselves doing laundry for quintuplets and do-it-yourself re-modelers who add restrooms, sinks or lawn sprinklers without considering the ill effects to an existing septic system.

The earth can be looked at like a huge sponge. Like a sponge it can absorb a great deal of moisture but there is always a limit to its capacity. Torrential rainfall can flood a lateral line area that was previously dissipating its effluence as envisioned and create a river of very bad news for everyone downstream. Nature can also step in and cause the ground to shift, which throws the once level lateral lines out of kilter and their contents will collect at one end forming an offal oasis. Even freezing can stop absorption and allow sub irrigation to surface.

Rex had a tidy little business on the side performing "perk tests" required by the state to be conducted by licensed Health Inspectors prior to the installation of septic systems. A hole is drilled in the projected lateral line area and filled with water. The water is then timed to see how long it takes for it to percolate into the ground. If all goes well the hole won't hold water and the results will be used to design the system. Operating solely outside of Bliss city limits Rex became tight with the county boys who steered work his way. Eventually when a system would fail for whatever reason it was the perk test guy that everyone looked at first to take the fall and Rex abandoned the practice for health and sanity reasons.

Being assigned a septic complaint was always best in the summertime. Granted the smell would be worse than in winter, but locating the problem was usually a no-brainer. Older homes on huge lots were common culprits. By May the oppressive Texas heat would have turned the surrounding grounds brown except for a lush green patch not far from the house. If the problem had gone on long enough there might even be cattails or a conspicuous willow tree flourishing in the rising nutrients. If long-legged wading birds were present, the offending septic system had been allowed to see the light of day for way too long.

It was a blistering August day and by late afternoon all three inspectors had found urgent paperwork to keep them busy inside their miniscule but air-conditioned offices. Pam's phone could be heard by all of us and we dreaded getting the transferred call that would mean going back out in the oppressive heat and humidity so close to quitting time. She put the call through to Rex, and we breathed a collective sigh of relief.

Moments later the false sense of getting through another day was broken. Rex bellowed for Jocko to come into his office and he groaned when he got up to comply. Bruce and I let out a little chuckle at Jocko's bad luck. This turned out to be a huge mistake as Rex added, "Bring Ross with you."

Rex had been laboring over a pile of Critter Control reports and the doings in doggy land must have been worse than usual because the cloud of smoke that filled his office was impressive even for him. He handed Jocko a pink phone message with his illegible scribbling on the back and the address, phone number and complainant's name Pam had jotted down on the front. Jocko glanced at the slip of paper and groaned again. He was going through one of his bulked-up periods and he was prone to groan a bunch.

Rex pulled the last cigarette from a pack in his shirt pocket, crushed the pack and laid it next to two he'd already depleted on the desk near his heaping ashtray. He lit his cigarette with relish, took a long drag and spoke while exhaling, "Look you two. I've got a dog at the pound that supposedly bit a kid and it belongs to Councilwoman Grace. She's not a bit amused by the fact that the dog has to be quarantined and she thinks I should let her take it home and place it under house arrest. The fact that it's been picked up roaming the streets five times this month doesn't seem to have any bearing on her opinion."

Rex took another long drag and we waited in the smog for him to explain why that mattered to us. He pointed at the note, "That's a septic complaint on the new church they just built on State Road 121. The guy who owns the lot next door called it into Councilwoman Grace's office. She was quick to let me know that she attended services there and we just approved and passed the new construction of that system. I don't need her panties in any tighter of a knot than they already are over this dog thing so take care of this without a crap storm."

It was 102 degrees when Jocko and I walked out the back door and I volunteered to drive because I knew he wouldn't run the air-conditioning in his truck. We both knew that in this kind of heat we weren't going to encounter people that were happy to see us pull into the church's parking lot. Hot days and hot tempers have a way of colliding.

Junior Jones was waving at us from his side of the barbed wire fence that separated his place from the church's property when we wheeled into the lot. How such a crabby old man could still go by the name Junior was beyond me, but I'd handled more than my share of problems with Mr. Jones in the past and I knew there would be more to come.

Jocko had reviewed and approved the plans for the church's septic system. The city sewer lines had not come out this far yet and the church stood mostly alone except for a small group of houses scattered at the foot of a long slope on Jones' side of the fence. Jocko said between huffs as he labored to walk in the heat, "I believe Junior is standing right about midway on that side of the lateral lines. I'd have sworn that area was solid trees when they put that system in a few months ago."

As we got closer to the maniacally waving Junior I said, "You're right, but not only are all the old oak trees gone, it looks like most of the earth has been carted off as well."

We were joined from behind by Pastor Pleasance, who must have seen us from the big bay window in his rectory and rushed out to defend the church from whatever skirmish Junior had caused to summon two Bliss Health Inspectors. The portly pastor was perspiring profusely through a white dress shirt, and he could have wrung a cup of sweat from his silk tie by the time we reached the fence. Jocko had lathered up on our short saunter, but I'm sure his prolific perspiration was more chemically induced than the good reverend's.

Junior chose to forego any formal pleasantries and began screaming and pointing at Pastor Pleasance while we were still a few paces from a face-to-face confrontation. Junior had an irritatingly screechy voice and a lot of spittle sprayed our way as he shrieked, "You stinking Bible toters are killing off my catfish!"

This was an unexpected revelation, but looking past Junior a few feet I could see where the ground had been excavated to form a large tank that was only partially filled with scummy water. Festering in the relentless sun on the muck's surface were several dozen dead catfish.

Junior continued to fill in the blanks, "Your gosh dang septic system is poisoning my business. I want it stopped right now!"

Jocko held the upper and center strands of barbed wire apart, and I stepped through the fence to get a closer look. Sure enough, the unmistakable sign of effluent from the adjacent septic system was oozing through the newly cut embankment creating a path of moisture that ran downhill to the pond. The effluvium factor was markedly more noticeable on this side of the divide. Being ever helpful, Jocko pointed out, "That ain't holy water running out of there!"

Jocko didn't look very steady, but he managed to stare Junior down and asked, "Mr. Jones, when did you knock down all your trees and dig that big pit?"

Junior shot back, "This here is my land and I got every right to build a catfish farm on it if I want."

Jocko rolled his eyes and replied, "That's not the point, Mr. Jones. What we need to determine here is whether or not your digging and lumberjacking caused the problem or if the church is at fault." That was pretty quick thinking for a man that I was sure would pass out any minute.

Junior started to speak, but his mouth just sort of opened and closed like one of his dying catfish gasping for life. I took the opportunity to engage Pastor Pleasance in the conversation, "Pastor has the church changed anything since your septic system was installed."

He was quick to respond, "Why, no. Not that I can think of."

I pointed out, "There sure are a lot of cars here for a Tuesday afternoon. Is there some type of special service or meeting today?"

The pastor said, "No, that's just parents coming to pick up their children from our day care."

The pastor's answer breathed new life into Jocko and he wheeled on the preacher, "Did you say day care? There was no day care listed in the septic plans for this church. When did you start a day care?"

The pastor attempted to look indignant as the sweat rolled

down his face and the top of his pants began to show signs of becoming waterlogged. "Why it was always our intention to provide a safe school for our children. We just didn't have the funds in the initial construction for the extra kitchen and toilet facilities needed."

Jocko smiled because he was officially off the hook for approving bad plans. Nothing currently affecting this project was remotely like the project Jocko had signed off on.

Junior recovered his indignation and yelled, "I knew it. Your Bible brats are the cause of all my problems."

I was certain that Junior's problems went way beyond any damage the church could ever send his way and felt compelled to point out, "Mr. Jones, I'm no expert on catfish ponds or their operation, but you can bet that I'll be doing some fact finding on the subject real soon. As for your land development in the city limits, I know the Engineering Department is going to want to have a look at what you've accomplished."

Jocko was ready to wrap up this phase of the operation and get out of the sun. Sounding very official he stated, "Obviously there will be a lot of explaining to do on both sides of this complaint. Mr. Jones, you can expect to hear from Engineering, and Pastor Pleasance, that day care of yours will need inspecting, permitting and probably a separate septic system to handle the loads. Gentlemen we are done for now."

That was it. The big man had spoken and was headed for my tiny truck before any of us could object. I had to wrestle my way back through the fence without help this time. I was glad to be getting out of the heat.

Junior was headed down the hill to his battered pickup truck and the good pastor was cooling down in the Lord's house when we rolled out of the lot. I turned to Jocko and said, "We didn't write anything up or get either one of them to sign our paperwork."

Jocko leaned back into his seat, closed his eyes and let the truck's air conditioning revive him. With a slight smirk he replied, "Now, you're learning, kid."

The Chief tells me that they've pumped over a million gallons of water on this thing already and it hasn't phased it.

CHAPTER 9
THE GREAT TIRE FIRE

Not long after Junior Jones' catfish farm went belly-up, I was called into the Chief's office to handle another from a long list of grievances Junior would file with the city. Rex's eyes were bulging beyond their normal range, and I knew that things at home weren't going that well for him. To add to the stress that the man seemed to heap upon himself, his wife had decided that they should move into a bigger house just outside the city limits of Bliss in a ritzy enclave called Lakeview Manors.

Rex handed me a complaint form that thankfully had been filled out by Pam when she took the call. He said, "Since you and Junior have become such fast friends, go out there across from his place and find out what he's bellyaching about this time. And by the way, what are you doing this Saturday?"

I'd been perusing the complaint form and was caught off guard by the Saturday question. I looked up at Rex and said, "Nothing special, why?"

Rex grinned slightly and answered, "Now it's purely on a

voluntary basis, but I'm asking all my inspectors if they would help me move this Saturday. We're only going a couple of blocks and I have a big utility trailer to haul stuff on."

How could I have been so stupid? Nothing is voluntary when the boss is asking and I agreed to help. Jocko was outside the Chief's door when I exited and he grinned while asking, "He got you too, huh?"

I replied, "You could have warned me."

Jocko shot back, "Are you kidding? No way it's just me and Bruce schlepping the Chief's crap."

I gave him a digital salute above my head as I walked out the back door with my complaint and Jocko was still laughing when the door closed behind me. According to Junior, hundreds of truckloads of used tires were being carted onto the property across the State Highway from his place. Junior didn't know what they were doing with all those old tires and he didn't like it one bit. When Junior's catfish farm wouldn't hold water he tried turning his giant pit into an illegal landfill and I was the one who was sent to point out the error in his latest scheme. It had cost him a lot more to clean up the mess than he ever got from dumping fees so we still weren't on hugging terms. Junior had learned all about the consequences of operating an illegal dump and was eager to see someone else get busted.

Several hundred acres belonging to the Ruselow Ranch sprawled out across the State Highway from Junior's small parcel. There was only one dirt road entrance and it was open with just a cattle guard for security. I knew the ranch was in the process of being carved up and sold off to developers, but no signs of surveying or construction were visible from the blacktop when I turned and headed for the modest ranch home a few hundred yards from the gate and down a long draw.

I could not believe my eyes when I stopped in front of the house. Piled in ten-foot stacks and covering the size of a football field were thousands of old tires. The Ruselows had moved out long ago and a renter came out of the house to see what I was up to. It was a bewildering sight and I did not speak to the man when he first approached me. He said, "Can I help you with something, mister?"

I turned to look at him next to me and said, "Where did all these tires come from?"

He shrugged his shoulders and replied matter-of-factly, "All over mostly. You'd be surprised what people will pay to get rid of them things. You need to unload some tires, mister?"

I said, "No, but you do. My name's Ross Ryan and I'm with the Bliss Health Department. Every single one of these tires has got to go to an approved dump. I can't believe there's so many of them. Do you own this property, Mr. uh, I'm sorry, what is your name?"

The man flashed me a multi-gapped grin and stuck his hand out, "I'm Jason Smith, but everyone calls me, "Weasel." Heck, we's just rentin' this place until we can get all these tires hauled off to where they cut 'em up in Oklahoma. You got a problem with that?"

"Yes, yes I do," I shot back while shaking the man's blackened hand. "You can't dump or store these tires here legally and they all have to go."

Weasel took off a severely soiled cap and scratched his matted hair while musing, "Well, by dang we got us a real bug tussle here. Ya see, I don't reckon they're quite ready to take all these here tires off our hands back in Oklahoma just yet. They're still working on the shreddin' plant and the storage yard."

"Mr. Smith, do the Ruselows know what you're doing down here?" I asked.

Weasel grinned and shook his head no. "I don't figure they much care. We ain't seen any of the owner's bunch since we moved in about six months ago."

I got a blank form out of my city vehicle and told Weasel while I was writing, "I'm going to have to notify the property owners to clean up this mess and the tires have to go and that's all there is to it. I need you to sign this form saying you've been notified."

Weasel glibly took my clipboard, signed the form and asked, "How long you figure we got to clear out all these tires?"

I informed him that, "You are in violation right now and could be fined every day that these things stay here, but my main objective is to get rid of them. The sooner you start hauling them away the better chance we have of not ending up in court over fines."

The mention of fines and courts didn't set well with Weasel. He scratched his chest while he asked me, "Are the police coming down here? 'Cause we can have a semi-trailer here tomorrow and start cartin' these things away, if that would keep it between just you and me. I'm going to need a little time to move this many tires."

Now we were getting somewhere. I said, "Mr. Jones, if you can show me in good faith that you are moving these tires out of here and not allowing any more to be dumped I'll work with you. I'm going to come back and check up on you every couple of days and there had better be some progress made in eliminating these piles."

Weasel stuck his grimy hand back at me and said, "Fair enough. We'll start movin' 'em out tomorrow." While he was speaking, a one-ton truck with stake sides and full of tires pulled up in a cloud of dust. Weasel waved them away and shouted, "I cain't take no more tires boys. You'll have to find another place to get rid of 'em." The truck left with no questions asked.

I made it a habit to swing by Weasel's place and check on his progress at least once a week. There was always a partially filled semi-trailer parked near the tires and it appeared that the piles were diminishing. Several months slipped by and I stopped checking on Weasel's progress. That proved to be one of the biggest mistakes of my city career and I believe I came as close to being fired as a city worker can get.

It was in the early fall and activity had really started to take off on the old Ruselow Ranch. Survey stakes were cropping up all over the place and big bulldozers had started carving up the land for new roads. I noticed the plume of thick black smoke on the south side of town while driving to work that morning, but didn't think much of it. That all changed as soon as I entered the jailhouse.

Rex yelled for me to get into his office before I even reached my desk. Jocko and Bruce were laying so low as to almost seem invisible. Pam had pulled my slim file on the Ruselow tire complaint and I spotted it on Rex's desk as soon as I entered his office. Rex looked up at me and said, "Is this all you've got on the Ruselow place?"

Oh crap, the Ruselow place. I'd forgotten all about it. I confessed, "That's all there is, Chief. They've been slowly trucking those tires away and I haven't been pressing them very hard."

Rex looked at me with dismay and said, "That's just great! I was hoping you had a lot more to show for this than one inspection form and a certified letter to the property owners. Some fool has gone and set all those tires on fire, Junior has already been by here this morning to show me how the ashes from the fire have ruined the paint on his truck and Dick is waiting for us in his office to come and explain why there is a conflagration on the south side of town."

What a rotten start to a perfectly good day. Even Pam had managed to make herself scarce and the spotlight was all mine. I shrugged my shoulders and said, "What do you want me to do?"

Rex stood up and killed the last half of his cigarette with one long drag that was so intense the ash didn't even fall off the butt. He picked up the file and said, "Let's go see the man," as he marched past me toward the back door.

The Fire Chief was sitting in front of Dick Darling's desk when we arrived, and the City Manager was shaking his head side-to-side slowly until he fixed his gaze on me as I eased inside the door. Dick never turned away when Rex handed him my file, and I wanted to be anywhere but there at that moment.

Dick said to me, "Somehow I knew it would be you this morning." Then he looked down to check out my feeble file, which didn't take long at all.

Staring back into my eyes he said, "So you knew about this situation for over six months?" I started to reply but he held his hand up to stop me and went on, "No, don't say anything to me until I'm finished. The Chief tells me that they've pumped over a million gallons of water on this thing already and it hasn't phased it. The soot falling out of the black plume you may have noticed on your way to work this morning is causing complaints from every homeowner within five miles of there and the dispatcher just radioed to say a news helicopter had arrived from a Dallas station to spread the good word. From the looks of this file all you've got to say for yourself is that it fell through the cracks. Does that pretty much sum it up?"

My throat was so tight it was all I could do to squeak out, "Yes, sir."

Seeing me squirm I believe Dick started to enjoy himself. "Do you at least know how to get in contact with the developers that bought this property?" he asked.

I lied and said, "Yes."

Dick grinned through clenched teeth and ordered me to, "Call these people and start making this problem go away right now! I want to know how you plan to solve this fiasco by noon. Now get out!"

I scampered down the hall to the tax office to locate which conglomerate had purchased the blazing parcel of Ruselow Ranch and caught my first break of the day. The paperwork on the transaction had just come into the assessor's office and all the addresses and phone numbers were current. I could have kissed her when the clerk handed me the copies, but I had some urgent calls to make in panic mode.

I hit the jackpot on my first call and got the project coordinator listed on the plans for the shopping mall that was slated for construction on the burning tract. He was watching live coverage of the fire in his office when he picked up the phone to hear me asking, "Are you the person I need to talk to about the tire fire in Bliss?"

Mr. Ronny Sterns had neglected to take a physical look at the now burning land when he agreed to head up the construction of Beagle Corporation's strip mall in Bliss and was indeed anxious to talk to me before his boss got wind of the fire. "Who is this and what can you tell me about our property?" he asked.

"My name is Ross Ryan, Mr. Sterns. I am the Bliss Health Inspector assigned to get your land cleaned up. Someone set thousands of tires on fire that were illegally dumped on your building site and our fire department has informed me that water is not going to put out this fire."

It was quiet for a few seconds and then Mr. Sterns replied, "This is not happening to me."

It was quiet again so I cut in, "Mr. Sterns, I assure you that the fire is real and we need to act fast because it's upsetting a tremendous amount of people."

Hearing that understatement Ronny Sterns shook himself out of shock and said, "Give me a number where I can reach you. We have teams that handle these types of situations. I'll be on the site this afternoon."

I gave him the information he requested and hung up the phone. This was an international company with vast resources and they were going to jump on this bomb immediately. For the first time today I felt like I just might get out of this mess without being drawn and quartered by Dick Darling.

I dashed off a quick memo for Pam to type up and give to the City Manager regarding Beagle Corporation's willingness to cooperate. I took a two-way radio and told Rex I was heading for the fire scene. Rex growled something about his ulcers, but I was rushing out the door and didn't want to hear another litany about how I was ruining his health. A giant black cloud could be seen trailing off in the soft breeze to the west from the fire's source as I drove toward the area. A second helicopter had been dispatched from Dallas to tell the world about my mistake. I could only hope that no reporters would show up to put my mug on television.

I flashed my big gold Health Inspector's badge to get past the security that had been set up at the entry gate. The circus that appeared at the foot of the hill as I drove down the slope was priceless. Several fire trucks were parked safely away from the raging blaze and I had no idea that Bliss had so many police officers. A group of Fire Department and Police brass were gathered around a tall man who looked totally out of place in his Armani suit. That had to be Mr. Ronny Sterns in the flesh holding court.

A police captain pointed at me as I approached the group and said, "That's Ross Ryan." Mr. Sterns turned immediately and walked toward me. Oh, man he was big and I was sure I was about to catch his full wrath.

Ronny Sterns stuck out his hand for me to shake and said, "Mr. Ryan, I believe we are well on our way to getting this mess resolved. I have a giant front-end loader in route that is the type used to fight forest fires. We plan to bury the tires until the fire is extinguished and avoid wasting any more water and creating tainted run off if you agree."

I could have kissed the man full on the lips. Did I agree? I tried to maintain some professional composure and replied, "That sounds fine to me."

Then it just got better. Mr. Sterns continued, "My people have located the rest of the discarded tires over that hill in two separate ravines. My engineer says that we can doze temporary roads to the tops of the ravines and remove the tires by hand for hauling if you can give us a few days to get the men and equipment in place."

I had never gone over that hill and looked into the ravines that I didn't even know were there. I had been so shocked by the amount of tires in front of the house and out in the open that it never even dawned on me to search the property for more. I mustered my straightest face and said, "I'll work with you on that, but you'll have to make sure this area stays secure."

Mr. Sterns smiled and said, "Believe me, Mr. Ryan, nobody wants to make sure this never happens again anymore than I do."

I watched as a monster tractor buried mounds of molten rubber and the operator worked well into the night under portable lights to complete the job. Nationwide Disposal had been contracted to stop the inferno and remove all the environmentally unsavory debris afterwards. They were real pros and bailed me out of my worst nightmare. That tire fire burned underground for a solid week and I was there every day to check on its progress and make sure the newly located tires didn't come back to haunt me.

I started keeping better records in my files after the tire fire. In nine more years of working for Bliss I never let another complaint "fall through the cracks."

Unwilling and untrained workers are not the best labor to tackle any type of job, but add unappreciated to the mix and disaster is imminent.

CHAPTER 10
MOVING THE CHIEF

Saturday morning was cold and a heavy mist hung in the air. There was no wind or the dismal day would have been a complete letdown. Jocko, Bruce and I arrived at Rex's house on the appointed hour and commiserated our sorry lot in the front driveway before going to the door to announce our presence.

Bruce started, "Man, this sucks!"

Jocko added, "This is the kind of morning made for staying in a warm bed with a good woman."

I walked toward the front door and replied to both of them, "We might as well get this show started. I don't relish being here all day." I rang the bell as the three of us forlornly loitered on the front porch.

Rex's preteen daughter answered the door with a bratty, "What do you want?" She was a demon child at that awkward age where her forehead appeared two times too tall for the rest of her face. She possessed a baby fat physique obtained by years of snacking her way through cartoons and sitcoms while lounging on the sofa.

Before I could answer The Dragon Lady, Rex's wife, materialized behind her evil offspring with a glazed donut in one hand and a lit cigarette in the other. She said, "We're still eating breakfast. I'd prefer for you boys to wait in the drive until we're finished." Without waiting for a reply she swung the door shut in our faces.

Unwilling and untrained workers are not the best labor to tackle any type of job, but add unappreciated to the mix and disaster is imminent. The three of us whirled around with every intention of driving away from this unwanted duty when Rex pulled up and began backing a long flatbed trailer into the driveway with his one-ton truck. We were trapped.

Rex did not look any happier than we were when he stepped out of the truck's cab and headed our direction. He said, "Thanks for coming. Did you guys just get here?"

There was no point in ratting out the Dragon Lady. A fight between her and the Boss would just prolong the day's agony. I replied, "Yep. Let's get cracking on this thing."

Rex led the way into his four-bedroom home. I had only been in there once before at a joint Christmas party that Rex and the Dragon Lady had thrown for the people they worked with. Not only did the city workers not meld well with the bank stiffs from his wife's camp, I managed to indulge in far too many spirits and let Rex prod me into telling his hated brother-in-law how atrocious his singing and guitar playing efforts were when he attempted to perform Christmas carols. The Dragon Lady was livid that night.

The Dragon Lady and her Evil Sister where drinking coffee, smoking and downing the last of the donuts at the kitchen table while both of their daughters watched a small television on the kitchen counter that faded in and out of a cloud of secondhand smoke. The Dragon Lady instructed Rex to, "Go ahead and get started in the den. We're almost done in here."

I looked around the house and it struck me that something was not right. Everything looked normal! Then it hit me, not one thing had been packed or readied for a move. This move had been planned for weeks and nothing was boxed up. My hopes of using at least part of my day off for myself were dashed.

Rex pointed at the back den and instructed us to, "Just pick up the big stuff first and set it on the trailer. We'll have to make several trips and maybe the girls will have some of the smaller stuff packed up by the time we get to it."

The Dragon lady yelled from the kitchen, "I heard that!"

Bruce and I picked up a small organ only to find out it weighed a ton. We set it down none too gently to rest several times while lugging it outside and nicked two walls in the process, but we got it to the trailer in one piece. We turned to see Jocko carrying a small magazine rack with nothing inside and he set it next to the organ in the front of the trailer.

Bruce and I took a large sofa from the back room next and repeated our haphazard nicking of walls on the way to the trailer. We tucked it snugly against the organ and Jocko showed up with a small footstool. Noticing a bad pattern forming I confronted Jocko, "Hey, muscle man, what's with you moving all the light stuff?"

Jocko chuckled and replied, "I don't carry anything heavy unless it has a weightlifting bar attached to it." He then proceeded to show me a long scar on his right elbow and explained, "I was helping a guy move a refrigerator when I was younger and dumber and tore the tendon when it slipped. No more moving heavy furniture for me." I had hoped it was a joke, but Jocko never carried anything that weighed over twenty-pounds the whole day leaving me, Bruce and Rex to do all the heavy lifting.

The flat trailer held a surprisingly large amount of furniture and we emptied the den and living room in less than an hour. We were ready to take the first load to the Flint's new love nest when Rex announced, "It's just a few blocks over there so why don't you boys ride on the trailer and steady things so we don't have to tie and untie the load?" Great, now we were human tie down straps.

Rex's new house wasn't much larger than his old place, but it was in a neighborhood with a decidedly higher tax bracket. We moved his stuff into the rooms where it would now live and headed back for a second load. The unloading process went smoother and faster than the loading ordeal as the new house had wider doors and hallways.

The Dragon Lady greeted Rex at the door with, "You S.O.B. You ran off and left me here for almost an hour with no cigarettes!" The Dragon Lady and her Evil Sister had cars, but they had loaded them with breakables piled into paper sacks for transport and didn't want to risk driving to the store with such delicate cargos. Rex unhooked his truck and went for cigarettes while we piled the second load on the trailer.

Bruce and I were carrying a large sofa from the back guest bedroom when the Demon Child and her cousin, who were blocking the hallway, stopped us. I asked her to please move and she shot back, "Can't you see we're playing here? You're just going to have to wait."

It was a good thing that I had my hands full of sofa, because I never wanted to strike a child so bad in all my life. Bruce was much cooler than I and said, "Get out of the way now or I will drop this sofa on your heads." The girls seemed to find that amusing and scampered off giggling.

The ladies and the girls left in the cars full of fragile items ahead of our second load and were at the new house when we arrived. This slowed the unloading process dramatically as the Dragon Lady insisted on having us place every piece of furniture we brought in exactly where she planned for it to stay after the move. I began to fully understand Rex's constant headaches and lack of desire to leave for home in the evenings after work.

Around 2:00 PM Jocko informed Rex that we were ready to take a break and get something to eat. The Evil Sister overheard this request and said, "Why you bunch of pansies. We're just getting started here. You don't need to be wasting time eating."

Jocko's face looked more strained than I'd seen all day and Rex chimed in, " How about I go pick up some hamburgers?" That sounded very good to all of us until the Dragon Lady added; "Keep the receipt so we'll know how much everybody owes." We ate our burgers in the driveway sitting on the trailer between loads and Rex treated. I don't think he told his loving wife.

I sat on a cheap microwave stand to keep it from falling off the trailer on one trip and broke a castor off the back corner. A garbage bag broke and Bruce dropped a load of clothes in the dirt on the new home's lawn. Jocko dropped a small radio on the pavement when the handle came loose. These trifles and many more were carefully concealed upon delivery for the happy new homeowners to discover long after we were gone.

We slunk away just after dark without telling Rex. Everything had been transported, but the Dragon Lady was inside giving orders on where to put away loose items like dishes and utensils. As I was driving off I heard her yell to Rex, "Have one of the boys start hanging pictures in the living room."

*I was stunned and the vacant eyes of dead deer staring up
at me was not helping.*

CHAPTER 11

BAM! BAM! BAMBI

Deer hunting in north Texas is a serious sport. Actually there are very few places to hunt deer in the immediate north Texas area, which is exactly the point. Manly men of every age, shape and cultural background rent deer leases or chip in together to buy deer hunting properties far away from their jobs, wives, families and homes. During the fall and early winter months of deer season, these men pack up their guns and grub and head for deer camps in droves.

Deer camps may be just that, tents or campers left at a central site on the property to be hunted or they can be old farmhouses or even nice cabins depending upon the budget of the hunters in the group. Men gather at these locations to drink, stink, eat whatever they want, play cards and tell lies while belching, farting and scratching without fear of female retribution. It is a rich tradition, steeped in lore, that Texas men introduce their sons to as soon as they are big enough to carry a rifle and old enough to know better than to tell what they witnessed while staying at a deer camp.

White-tailed deer populate most of Texas and are the main

prey. Texas whitetails are not renown for massive size and many appear to have been bred with jackrabbits. Nevertheless a rifle capable of taking down a rhinoceros must be purchased and fitted with a telescope that could clearly make out the flags left on our moon's surface to hunt whitetails. Several trips to a local gun range will be required to zero-in the scope after it has been mounted and bore-sighted on the new rifle. This will provide deer hunters with the opportunity to inspect each other's equipment and brag about their own while planning their next hunting expeditions.

Super serious sportsmen will allocate a week or two of their vacation time to travel to another state, like Colorado or Wyoming, to hunt mule deer. These safaris are justified because mule deer are far larger and more illusive game and the hunting conditions will be much more primitive and demanding of the hunter's skills. A four-wheel-drive vehicle may have to be purchased and maintained year round for this annual outing and the state permit for just one buck can run hundreds of dollars, but the hunter knows it's worth every penny.

The good hunter's wife will peck her man on the cheek and worry whether he has packed enough warm clothes to survive in the harsh outback he is bravely driving off to face with his comrades. In reality the boys may be booked into comfortable rooms and utilize guides to drive them around on groomed and stocked properties to pop some unsuspecting mule deer that was taking handouts from a ranch hand the week before deer season. The mighty hunter will return to his family with a picture of the packed and processed deer he has brought back on ice and stories of the hunt. He will be proud of the venison he has provided for his family. They probably can't stand venison's taste, and it will end up costing him somewhere around two hundred dollars a pound.

The debate over whether deer hunting is good or bad for the deer population rages constantly and is a great topic to keep hunters occupied during the off-season. Deer are accomplished breeders and anyone living in a rural environment with deer habitat will be happy to tell you personal stories of how their vehicles were wrecked by kamikaze deer or their gardens and crops were devoured by herds of the hungry varmints. I hunted in my younger days and killed my share of bucks, but woke up one day realizing that I wasn't mad at anything enough to want to shoot it anymore.

Taking down one of the fleet of foot, four-legged mammals may actually be anticlimactic to the hunt. The disgusting business of disemboweling or field dressing the slaughtered beast and dragging the carcass to a road where a vehicle can haul it back to camp is followed by the complication of keeping the meat chilled and protected from insects long enough to get it home for proper butchering. Should a hunter kill a deer during the first few days of a week-long trip, a warm spell will most surely set in and require a desperate search for ice or a packing house to save his meat.

Ye Olde Meat Shoppe was on my list for inspection and it had been a venerable market for quality meat purchases for as long as anybody could remember in Bliss. It was owned and operated by Clyde and Elmore Hackson who had learned the butchering trade in the army during World War II.

Clyde and Elmore had returned from the war and set up shop in a nondescript cement building with a tin roof. They were located near the oldest intersection in Bliss and the business had grown and prospered over the years. Giant walk-in coolers were added to the rear of the small building and a kitchen with a side office had been tacked to the back of the original main structure.

A meat-processing establishment would have fallen under the watchful eye of State Health Inspectors in days of yore, but the State of Texas had sloughed off all its inspection responsibilities within the city limits and now it was my job to visit the Hackson's. Rumor had it that the men were serving-up hearty lunches to the locals in their back kitchen add-on which also placed them under the restaurant rules.

I walked back to a time before my birth when I entered Ye Olde Meat Shoppe's front door. There was a thick layer of cedar shavings on the concrete floor and open coolers full of thickly sliced cuts of beef, pork and lamb formed a u-shaped barrier between the customers and the cleaver wielding men behind the counters.

Opening the door had tripped a tiny bell that tipped the butchers off to my presence. Clyde looked up from turning a massive ham into deli slices to say, "Watcha need?" His hands never stopped working and he turned his attention back to the business of slicing meat before I could give an answer. Elmore was at the far end of the room hacking up something with a band saw while a much younger male and one female employee seemed to constantly walk in and out of a large cooler to the back rooms carrying packages.

I announced that I was an Inspector with the Bliss Health Department and had come to perform their routine inspection. All activity ceased immediately and the only sounds heard were the tiny fans of the meat display coolers laboring to keep their contents cold. I stepped closer to the counter where Clyde had fixed me with a confused gaze and held up my inspector's badge. That brought him around.

Clyde turned off his deli slicer and asked, "Now just when the hell did this happen? Did someone turn us in for something or what?"

I said, "No. This is meant to be a routine health inspection just like every other food service establishment in Bliss gets bi-monthly. It shouldn't be much different than the ones the State has been conducting."

Elmore laughed loudly and broke the tension in the air. Everyone seemed to breathe easier. Elmore said, "Son, we ain't never seen no state inspector here or even give much thought to you guys down at the health department by city hall. I do recall them building inspection boys selling us some permits when we moved in this place, but that was a long time before you come along."

Clyde added, "I don't remember you ever coming in here and I know just about everybody who works for the city. Heck they all buy their meat from us and most of the old-timers come by on Fridays for our Bar-B-Q lunches."

Well that's just great, I thought to myself. Here's another pioneering effort working with a historical treasure endeared to the hearts of everybody in Bliss. Having learned some heavy-handed lessons from these types of situations I approached this one as gingerly as possible. I asked Clyde, "Would you mind if I poked around and took some notes? You guys don't have to stop a thing that you're doing and we'll talk about what I've found when I'm done and you have time."

Clyde replied, "That'll be fine, young feller. Make yourself to home." Elmore went back to his band saw and the two young assistants resumed moving packages wrapped in white butcher paper from place to place.

I walked into the back room and set my briefcase on one of the eight-foot folding tables no doubt used by the lunch club and went to work filling blank pages with small print full of violations.

Ye Olde Meat Shoppe was not that big, but time had not been kind to the structure and it was evident that not a lot of profit was being plowed back into the facility's upkeep.

I'd been working steadily when the men closed shop at 4:00 PM and began cleaning-up for the day. I did not relish presenting my long list of needed reforms to guys who cut up animals for a living.

The young lady from the front filled a large dish washing sink in the back room next to an ancient gas stove and oven. She began washing knives and cutting boards while the young man swept up wood shavings that had soaked up spilled blood and replaced them with fresh cedar chips.

Clyde stopped for a second before going into his office and asked if I was ready to talk yet. I said, "No. All that's left is the two big coolers and the small room connecting them behind your office."

"Suit yourself," says Clyde, "I'll be in here when you're ready."

I swung open a heavy wooden door that separated the main structure from the outer cooler enclosure and froze in my tracks. Scattered across a concrete floor in front of me were the carcasses of a dozen or more deer and Elmore was pulling a fresh one from the bed of a pickup that was backed into the entrance at the far end of the room. I was stunned and the vacant eyes of dead deer staring up at me was not helping.

Elmore shook the hand of a man dressed in camouflage fatigues and said, "I should have your venison ready in about a week." The man thanked him and drove away. Elmore shut the outer door and said, "I hate deer season," as he walked past me and back into the main building. I, too, suddenly hated deer season.

I made my way around the carnage on the floor and opened

the first of the two large walk-in coolers. Another dozen or so deer carcasses hung inside, but these had their hooves, heads and hides removed and looked like smaller versions of the cow and pig carcasses that accompanied them. The same scene repeated itself in cooler number two. I'd seen enough for the day and hesitantly went in to confront the Hackson brothers.

Clyde motioned for me to come into the office. I sat in an old easy chair across from his desk and Elmore came in and sat on a small sofa. I turned to the first page of my copious notes and began, "I realize this place is old and there is a lot of rust on equipment, cracked walls and floors, damaged ceiling tiles and preparation surfaces that need refinishing. But I have to admit that you keep your shop as clean as can be expected with what you have to work with and I didn't find a single cooler or piece of meat that was not being kept at or below the required temperature. Well, that is except for those deer laying in front of the outer coolers."

Elmore shifted his weight on the sofa and said, "I hate deer season."

I was pleased to see Clyde smile before he told me, "I called Rex while you were poking around in the back room. Ole Rex has been a regular around here since we got started and usually makes it to lunch on Fridays. He told me to listen to what you had to say because you knew what you were doing, but don't expect me to start jumping through no hoops."

I don't know why I felt relieved to hear Clyde say that, but I was. I looked him straight in the eye and said, "OK. Let's just start by addressing the things that are way out of step with the current requirements and we'll consider the rest of the structural stuff a work in progress."

Clyde chuckled and said, "Dang, boy. I think I'm goin' to like you."

I managed to get the Hackson brothers to dedicate one of their outside coolers to wild game only during hunting season and keep all the USDA inspected meats separated. Elmore thought that was a brilliant idea. Neither of them liked dressing deer, but they felt they had to keep doing it out of loyalty to their older customers.

Wearing hair restraints rubbed the men the wrong way, but when I said that baseball caps would meet the requirement they agreed to give it a try. Clyde decided that they could have caps made up for sale to customers while they were at it.

Since they were running a limited restaurant of sorts, one of them would have to acquire a current food preparation certificate. Both men were quick to point out their army training to which I replied, "Then you should have no trouble at all passing the required course." They weren't pleased, but did not argue. I agreed to let them put off taking classes until the influx of dead deer subsided.

To my surprise the biggest brouhaha we dealt with was over removing the wood shavings from the cutting floors. Elmore informed me that, "Them is special wood shavings made just for that very purpose and I ain't ever worked in a shop, military or civilian, that didn't have shavings on the floor."

Clyde added, "It ain't safe to walk around on a bloody floor with sharp instruments without shavings. It just ain't. We replace the ones with big spills on 'em every day an sweep 'em all out and bleach the floor at the end of the week before new ones go down on Mondays."

I had to get help from the State Health Department on the wood shaving issue before I could get the Hacksons to see that cleaning a spill as soon as it happened was much more sanitary and safer than letting some of the splatter and dropped meat lay on their floor for an entire week. They finally came around, but I was reminded of how much they missed those wood shavings every time I set foot in their store.

Ye Olde Meat Shoppe was never perfect, but it was constantly improving. I wouldn't hesitate to buy meat from Clyde or Elmore, and without a doubt it's the finest place I know to unload a freshly killed deer carcass for processing.

I thought of all the tickets I could have written for not washing dishes and utensils properly, unsanitary food handling and temperature violations in the past, but here I was getting all John Wayne over the back door gaping open.

CHAPTER 12
CHINESE FIRE DRILL

By no means is it my intention in this chapter, or any part of this book for that matter, to be so unpolitically correct as to slander, libel or cast any dark aspersions on any particular peoples, places, ethnicities or personal persuasions. That's the honest to gosh truth in disclaimer form. I am attempting to relate events as I experienced them from my own unique vantage point, which admittedly is skewed due to being limited by only drawing upon north Texas circumstances.

Whether it occurred at the dinner table or some other polite social setting, when a person recovered from the surprise of meeting an authentic health inspector the first question they would ask me would be regarding the worst case of restaurant filth I'd ever encountered. After seven years of popping into eatery back doors I could report without reservations that the Chinese restaurants I inspected suffered from the greatest lack of fastidiousness.

Since I have not been into every Chinese kitchen in the world, I can only say that I never had any luck with the ones I inspected.

The Chinese kitchen employees in Bliss lacked the personal rapport with soap and water that health inspectors are wont to demand. One restaurant owner explained to me that in China food and clean water are often scarce and therefore never wasted. He added that Chinese people tended to place a high value on day-to-day survival and to them tossing out leftovers or constantly washing hands and utensils could mean going without eating and drinking the next day. While I could sympathize with his cultural quandary, I could not condone serving spoiled food in a soiled environment.

My first cultural clash with the Chinese method of handling food and practicing personal hygiene came days before my first Chinese New Year on the job. I drove up behind the Magic Wok restaurant and scattered dishwashers and bus boys like chickens in a barnyard as they fled inside from under and around a dilapidated Toyota. They scurried straight from replacing the rusted car's transmission past me standing with briefcase in hand at the back door and returned to their kitchen duties of preparing food and washing dishes with no thoughts of stopping by the hand wash sink for even the tersest of rinsing.

Normally I would have rounded them all up, escorted them to the cobwebbed hand-washing sink and expounded on the virtues of a good scrubbing prior to handling food and utensils but I was transfixed by a sight above the propped-open rear door that still haunts me. Attached to the inside doorframe at one end and the outer top edge of the door at the other was a piece of clothesline. Dangling by their necks in the 80-degree afternoon sun were several ducks. The quack was not long gone from these fowl, but they were rapidly building an impressive stench. I was dumbfounded by the spectacle of this multiple bird lynching.

My expression of puzzlement when the owner materialized caused her to launch into the following explanation without being asked. "Tees ducks for Chinese Nude Year. Day stay 'til bodies fall off heads. Then they ready for cook. Good, yes?"

My head swayed involuntarily from side-to-side and out came, "No, no, no, no, no!"

She knitted her brow and asked, "You no like duck?"

I replied, "That has nothing to do with it. You can't let these things rot until they fall apart and then serve them."

She laughed a little and said, "You kid-a-me, right. It bad joss no have duck for Nude Year."

I looked her directly in the eyes and said, "You're joss is in grave jeopardy then, because I will not allow you to serve these ducks to your customers. Where did they come from?"

She squared her shoulders and glaring up from her four-foot frame gave me a serious squint before replying, "You no kill my joss! Tees ducks for family not customers. My boyfriend shoots them."

I could not have been happier. With a slight chuckle I instructed her to, "Take them home immediately and do not bring them back to this restaurant. You must not mix unapproved foods with inspected products, please."

This made her happier and she yelled for one of the dishwashers to whisk away the offending birds. He took them down, loaded them into the trunk of a car that had been roasting in the direct sun and drove away. I could only hope they didn't return.

I've seen shrimp thawed in the mop sink, rice dried outside on air conditioning units, weevils sifted out of flour before using it, and raw chickens piled unprotected on the kitchen floor waiting to be cut-up. All of these sins committed right before my eyes while the perpetrators were on their best behavior during my inspection.

The violation that really takes the rice cake came on a rainy morning while I was sorting through a rodent infested portable building that had been set up behind the Zen Café to warehouse the restaurant's bulk food supplies. Using a mini flashlight I was peering into the gash made for an opening in the top of a five-gallon tin can of almonds. The almonds seemed animated and I poured a few onto a serving tray being used as the lid on a canister of flour. Roaches from inside the almonds scattered in the dim day's light.

I handed the can to the owner, who had been nervously shuffling from one foot to the other behind me and instructed him to, "Please go throw these in the dumpster."

His mouth gaped open in disbelief and he said, "You no understand. These very expensive almonds from China. They OK. We fix before serving to customers."

Having spurred my curiosity I replied, "By all means, show me how you fix these almonds for serving."

With a great flourish he dumped several cups of the lively almonds onto the same serving tray I had used and shooed away a dozen or so roaches. He then carefully plucked out several roaches that had foundered while feasting on the exotic nuts and tossed them aside. The almonds were then poured into a large colander, which hung on a nail protruding from the wall nearby, and swirled around until all visible clingy bits fell away. With a huge smile of satisfaction he held them up to me and said, "You see. Good as new."

I cannot describe the disappointment in his eyes when I was not impressed by his efforts. I made him pour bleach into the almond can before watching him toss it into his dumpster to dissuade him from the temptation of retrieving them after I left.

Once I had a Chinese owner whose kitchen had rats. When I brought this to his attention for immediate remediation I discovered during my follow-up inspection that he had brought in several cats to solve the problem. The same owner had experimented with raising live chickens in the ceiling tiles above his kitchen. When a 911 caller reported screaming that sounded like a murder in progress coming from this restaurant I responded with the police. We arrived to find the kitchen splattered with blood and scattered utensils as a result of a struggle that took place while the owner attempted to butcher a live hog. I made every effort to discourage this particular owner's future restaurant ambitions and attempted to steer him into a farming career.

Having responded to far too many complaints at The Noodle Noshery, I made a habit of swinging by their back door when working in the area. Unbeknownst to the patrons luxuriating in the cool dining room The Noodle Noshery's Chinese owner saved money by not air conditioning his kitchen during the blistering hot Texas summers, which prompted his kitchen staff to keep the back door propped open. With no screen to cover the gaping hole swarms of flies and mosquitoes made their way into the food preparation areas from the adjacent drainage ditch. My demands to keep the door closed or install a tightly sealed screen were ignored by the owner and his sweltering staff.

Furthering my exasperation with this crew was their complete lack of regard for proper kitchen decorum. Occasionally

I could get them to wash their hands, but I had reprimanded these same kitchen employees so many times for smoking and drinking while preparing food and washing dishes that I promised them each a personal citation of their very own if I caught them breaking the rules during any future inspections.

A mere four days after completing The Noodle Noshery's routine bi-monthly inspection, I pulled up behind the restaurant to find the back door propped open with a broken chair. A halfhearted effort had been made to install a screen door which now leaned against the dumpster several feet away. It was only an hour before the lunch rush so there were no sentries posted to warn the others of my stealth approach.

I was spotted first by the dishwasher as I entered the back door and he quickly spat his lit cigarette into the sudsy water in front of him. This seemed like such a good idea to the bus boy that he added his own smoke to the foamy water.

A very large man sat at the end of the wash sink's drain board sweating profusely while reducing a pile of raw chickens to bite-size chunks with a cleaver. The cigarette that dangled from his lower lip stayed put until he bumped it with the glass he retrieved from its nest among the chicken pieces while attempting to take a drink and fix me with a vacant stare at the same time.

A second bus boy wheeled in a cloud of smoke and retreated back into the dining room from whence he came immediately upon espying me at the back entry to warn the owner of my arrival. This commotion caused the cook to turn away from his woks with a drinking glass in hand and a freshly lit cigarette in his mouth to see why the bus boy had fled. The cook was so flustered that he put his cigarette out in a small saucepan by his prep table and nervously lit another one without thinking.

The Noodle Noshery's owner breezed into the kitchen all smiles and handshakes to welcome me to his establishment. I was livid. Using my right arm to perform a dramatic sweeping motion around the kitchen I proclaimed, "That's it! I am writing every person in this kitchen a citation. I've had it with you people this time. No more mister nice guy."

The stifling heat in the fetid kitchen and my elevated blood pressure created a slight buzz in my head. I could barely hear the owner plead with me as I moved to the far end of the kitchen by the dining room entry door and sat my briefcase on a low stool, which was the only clean spot I could find. I rummaged through my briefcase to locate my citation book while the owner whined, "Pleese no tickets. We do better, you see. You right. We do wrong, but that stop now. You always right. We ready to listen. No need for tickets."

I found my seldom used citation book and turned around to face the soon to be cited violators. To my surprise there was not a single soul left in the kitchen, save for the owner and me. I ran out the back door and looked both ways up the alley and down the drainage ditch, but there was no sign of my Chinese malefactors. They'd vanished. I couldn't believe it. They just ran away.

I went back into the kitchen to find the owner had put on an apron and started preparing lunch. He was busily working away at his woks when I stopped him to ask, "Where did they go?"

With a perfectly benign expression he replied, "Who?"

I said, "Oh, come on, you know who. Your kitchen help, that's who."

He turned to stir a huge wok of rice and said, "Just me here to get lunch ready."

I went into the dining room to cool off and the owner's wife was the only other employee in the restaurant. She was seating her first patrons of the day and acted like I was not there. Back into the kitchen I went and told the owner, "You're not getting out of this that easy. I'm writing you a ticket."

He looked up from his woks and said, "For what you write me a ticket? I no do nothing."

City citations have to be specific and have to be written to an individual. I did not want to face Sheila Swift in court and have to explain how I wrote this man a ticket for having nasty employees. I looked around the empty kitchen and grasped at the only thing I could think of that had been documented countless times and the owner could be held directly responsible for and told the owner, "I'm writing you a ticket for leaving the back entry open and unprotected from insects."

The owner set his rice off the fire, wiped his hands on his pants and said, "OK, you got me on that one."

I opened my citation book and said, "I'll need your driver's license to copy down your information."

He smiled his benign smile and said, "I no have driver's license."

I said, "Then I'll need your official identification card or passport or something."

He replied, "I no have that stuff here. You come back tomorrow maybe."

I said, "No. You are getting a citation today and maybe another one tomorrow if I return and that back door is still open. Now what kind of I.D. do you have? How do you drive to work without a driver's license?"

He smiled and nodded his head yes while answering, "Ah, my wife, she drive me."

I was so frustrated at this point that the whole mess began to turn humorous in my head. I could not back down, but I wanted to laugh out loud at how ludicrous the situation had become. I had no procedures for writing a person without an I.D. a ticket. Then it hit me and I asked, "Does your wife own this business with you?"

He looked confused for the first time and replied, "Yes, she number one partner."

I hated to do it, but it was my only way out. I said, "Then I'm afraid I'm going to have to write her the ticket."

The owner retrieved his wife from the dining room and she produced her driver's license so I could write her a ticket for leaving the back door open to their food preparation area. I thought of all the tickets I could have written for not washing dishes and utensils properly, unsanitary food handling and temperature violations in the past, but here I was getting all John Wayne over the back door gaping open. She took the ticket and thanked me.

I returned to The Noodle Noshery several times searching for the disappearing kitchen crew, but I never saw them again. It occurred to me later that those guys might not have been on the best of terms with the United States immigration folks and a binding summons to court would not have been in their best interest. I'm still impressed by their vanishing act. The restaurant owner seemed to have little difficulty replacing his lost help.

I have many more stories of mishaps in Chinese kitchens, but tales of this ilk should only be related in low doses. The human body is a remarkable machine and capable of processing some pretty strange stuff, but I still can't eat in Chinese restaurants to this day.

There among a cloud of loose feathers was a half-naked
man having sexual relations with a live chicken.

CHAPTER 13

ANIMAL HOUSE

On top of his duties as Chief Health Inspector, Rex Flint was
also responsible for overseeing The Bliss Animal Control Division.
His head animal control officer, Pamela Powers, who everyone
referred to as "Perky" when she was not around, generated many
of Rex's most monstrous headaches. Animal control officers were a
mixed lot of would-be policemen, tenured city employee's relatives
and former military personnel. They were people with a heart of
gold that could rescue a stranded duckling from being swept through
a sewer grate in the morning and perform euthanasia on a litter of
kittens that afternoon. Their ability to care or kill according to the
demands of the situation set them apart from most folks.

As the new City Manager, Dick Darling made it a point to
tell Rex, "The biggest problems and source of complaints in any city
are weeds and dogs." Initially Rex felt that the new City Manager
was empathizing with his plight. As it turned out, Dick was putting
Rex on notice that he was well aware of the problems that he faced
and expected Rex to keep them from escalating to his level.

When Jocko Marks joined the Bliss Health Department, Rex was anxiously searching for a way to fade the heat he constantly felt from Animal Control antics. Jocko's insistence that he had dealt directly with pet pains while employed by Demon County's Health Department made him an easy target. Bruce and I wanted no part of the circus that performed daily at the Critter Care Center and were more than happy to step aside and let Jocko take the reins. We were sure that the few extra shekels doled out for administrating dog pound doings fell short of compensating for the added stress.

The Critter Care Center was located at the termination of a dead end road near the edge of town. It was surrounded by swampy land that the Waste Water Treatment Plant utilized to spread their sludge for drying when the ghastly goo reached unmanageable proportions in the city's giant aeration vats. Countless animals of every description had been buried on the grounds after being incarcerated at the shelter and then exceeding their stays of execution. Compounding the fug of the ambient air was the daily accumulations of animal excrement. I detested having to visit the place and could not fathom how the people who toiled there ever became accustomed to the reek.

Maintaining full staff levels at the dog pound was a constant quest. People who loved animals but could not bring themselves to dispatch them from this world when they were no longer wanted didn't last long on the job. When overtime hours exceeded the allowable budget tolerances, Rex would press his salaried health inspectors into filling the gaps. I had been sent to provide just such a service one evening and as usual was expected to perform my new task with little or no training. I would be driving the mosquito spray truck on a hot June night when nobody else was available.

The size and ferocity of Texas mosquitoes is legendary. Tales of the blood-sucking parasites swooping down in swarms to carry off livestock or completely siphon off the vital fluids of unsuspecting prey are passed on to each new generation of campers, hikers, sportsmen or anyone partaking in outdoor activities. A rainy May, followed by a steamy June, would most certainly guarantee a bumper crop of the itty-bitty vampires.

Bliss's mosquito spray rig, which was mounted on the back of a dilapidated half-ton pickup, was a relic. When the temperamental machine functioned correctly, a massive plume of white fog spewed from a silver cannon-like tube that was attached to a metal box, which contained an air compressor. Thirty-gallons of ordinary diesel fuel were mixed with a couple of cups of Malathion to create a lethal cloud that could hang in the air for ten- to fifteen-minutes on a still day or gently waft across an entire neighborhood when borne on a light breeze. The diesel created the smoke and supposedly caused the Malathion to cling to whatever it floated into contact with and leave a deadly residue for the tiny tormentors.

The majority of entomologists versed on mosquito control methods have concluded that the effectiveness of using such a sprayer is minimal because the amount of poison that can be safely distributed by this type of fogging is miniscule. However, the psychological benefits of seeing a cloud of mosquito killing mist envelope an infested area is huge.

Folks who lacked the financial resources to seal up their homes and rely on central air conditioning to keep them comfortable inhabited the first neighborhoods I drove into with my mosquito slaying rig. Homeowners languishing on well-worn sofas and easy chairs with exposed stuffing occupied almost every porch on every block. These residents actually cheered as I slowly inched down their street and many implored me to tarry in front of their domiciles to allow my fogger to amass an extra-thick cloud of killing vapors.

In the upscale enclaves of Bliss, people shot me the finger or screamed in derision as they darted outside to check the progress of meat cooking on grills or adjust their water sprinklers before heading back into their air conditioned homes. Several indignant citizens charged into the street to flag me down and demand an account of exactly what was in the noxious haze I was spreading. It was an exhausting ordeal.

Just before dark, as I was getting ready to call it a day and return to the Critter Care Center, I noticed a young boy on his bicycle in my rearview mirrors merrily darting in and out of the thick jet of fog streaming from my sprayer. This lad pulled alongside my open window when I stopped for the sign at the end of his street.

The boy beamed up at me and asked, "Mister can that stuff hurt me?"

Not being very child oriented I replied, "Kid, that smoke will kill ya!" I can still see him pedaling furiously into the night wailing for his mommy.

My great mosquito massacre generated a record number of calls the next day, both pro and con. I was never asked to operate the contrary contraption again and its use was phased out completely the following year.

Perky was ambitious and promiscuous according to the Bliss grapevine, which could spread the news that you had spit before it could hit the ground. Perky's alleged escapades drove Rex batty and he had all his inspectors on high alert as we went about our daily duties looking for her vehicle parked in front of some tryst nest while she was supposed to be on the job. This book is not about to become a tell all at this point, which I'm sure will cause many readers to breathe much easier. It's not that Bliss couldn't hold its own with the Peyton Places in this sordid world; I prefer to leave the steamy stuff covertly indulged in to the writers of bodice rippers.

Perky found herself a higher paying position in another city and Rex gave her a glowing recommendation. A big Samoan named,Tiki Bao, who had a wife and a houseful of kids to keep him busy when he wasn't diligently handling the humane concerns of the city, replaced her. Tiki and Jocko became close cohorts and Jocko began using the Critter Care Center as a frequent refuge from the constant stream of calls that flowed into his office.

Normal complaints involving escaped animals or noisy pets didn't raise much interest at the Health Department for most of us, but a chicken sent us all out to the Critter Care Center one morning. During the wee hours of the day, when people's judgments tend to get clouded by alcohol, drugs or fatigue, a patrolman on the night shift happened upon a man in a pickup truck parked by the lake. Not an unusual occurrence, but he drew the officer's attention for being in a city park that had closed hours earlier.

Cautiously approaching the suspect pickup the officer observed a wild struggle in progress. Due to the intensity of the exertion in the truck's cab, the driver never noticed the officer until he was at the window shining a large flashlight into the fray. There among a cloud of loose feathers was a half-naked man having sexual relations with a live chicken. The hen was none too happy about the whole affair and had inflicted multiple scratching and pecking related wounds on the fowl rapist. The whole bloody mess was a surreal spectacle.

The man was promptly carted off to the hoosegow and the chicken interned at the dog pound. Rex, Bruce, Jocko and I were compelled to drive out to the Critter Control Center to see for ourselves what could possibly make a hen romantically irresistible. Other than looking tired and severely irritated, we could find no alluring qualities in the bird, but it made great grist for future jokes and bad puns.

Let's all get buck naked and sit as still as statues while we sail by. That ought to liven up those old gals.

CHAPTER 14
BLISS LAKE
◆◆◆

The State of Texas has no naturally occurring lakes, except for a sprawling cypress swamp along the Louisiana border. To provide the water resources demanded by a large population, dams are constructed across major watershed drainage areas to create reservoirs and then promptly named after the legislators responsible for getting the finances appropriated for these public works projects.

The Army Corps of Engineers immediately assumes all power over the building and maintenance of Texas reservoirs. The Corps controls every aspect of development on, in or around its reservoirs. Property owners buying land that abuts Corps controlled areas must seek permission to alter their parcels in any way that the Corps might view as having an impact on the reservoir including tasks as trivial as trimming a tree that is growing on Corps Land but hangs over private property.

Gonzales-Little Oak Reservoir was created in the 1950s. It was not large by Texas' standards, but became a huge boon to the town of Little Oak and spurred the growth of nearby Little Dallas. As the Dallas Metroplex area expanded exponentially in the ensuing years, a much larger dam was built in Bliss to create a reservoir that contained roughly 150,000 surface acres. A hole was dynamited in the Gonzales-Little Oak's dam and the two lakes became one with Bliss swooping in to claim naming rights and dubbing the conjoined waters, Lake Bliss.

Lake Bliss was deepest at the new dam, but a third of the lake contained submerged trees in thick stands just below the water's surface. Another third was so shallow that when the water level dropped dramatically, it required no god-like powers to walk across the reservoir. The lake was never clear, but a windy day could whip the waters and stir the sediment from the bottom giving the lake an ocher hue. The Corps was charged with guessing how much water to release from the reservoir to counter anticipated droughts or floods, and it was agreed upon by almost all of the recreational users of the lake that they rarely got it right. This kept the local boat and motor repair shops busy fixing hulls that had run aground and engines that had struck submerged objects.

It was common knowledge among area health professionals that the little towns, which sprang up around the lake, grew faster than their infrastructure. They all released raw sewage directly into the already turbid lake when deluges overwhelmed their meager wastewater treatment plants. I made it a point not to swim in Lake Bliss or eat fish that had been taken from it, but that did not stop thousands of unsuspecting water enthusiasts from swimming, water skiing, boating and fishing in the reservoir.

With all the willy-nilly ups and downs of the lake's level, the water along the shoreline was constantly flooding or retreating. The perpetual flushing and filling created beaches of sand, sandstone, clay or rock depending on where the water lapped at the moment.

Several marinas operated on Lake Bliss. They all incorporated floating docks that could rise and fall with the lakes fickle water levels. Severe drought conditions could cause the marinas to end up on dry land or force them to detach their docks from pilings and temporarily drag them for anchoring in deeper waters outside their respective coves.

The fluctuating nature of the lake deterred most businesses from setting up shop at the water's edge, but The Angler's Hideaway had been an ongoing concern on Lake Bliss for as long as anybody could remember. The Angler's Hideaway was a conglomeration of wooden platforms that floated on fifty-five-gallon steel drums. The platforms were anchored to the bottom and tied to the shore by thick steel cables.

The central portion of the Hideaway's floating cluster was completely enclosed. Several large rectangular openings in the floor allowed people to sit around them and fish inside where they were protected from the elements. The adjoining Fish O Rama Restaurant had fallen on hard times over the years, but the kitchen still operated as a snack bar for hungry anglers. Faded Polaroid snapshots of giant catfish, carp and crappie were thumb tacked to a crumbling cork board just inside the drafty entryway showing the trophies hauled from the murky depths beneath the Hideaway. The place reeked like an old shrimp boat and the inherent funk peaked when the odor of dead fish mingled with the greasy aromas emanating from the grill on a hot summer day.

Spring rains had filled Lake Bliss to a record high level and the red sand and gravel parking lot was mostly under water when I arrived to perform my first inspection at The Angler's Hideaway. A few battered pickup trucks and station wagons lined the edge of the flood waters, and a temporary walkway leading to the ramp at the front door had been constructed of old tires, cinder blocks, two-by-fours and plywood.

After picking my way along the precarious bridge I entered the open front door to find most of the day's dozen or so patrons gathered around the center fishing well. They were old men with leathery skin that had been ravaged by age and the sun. Most wore dingy, white undershirts, which exposed withered tattoos that had become giant blotches of indistinct black on their arms and backs.

These men were yelling instructions as they ebbed and flowed along the sides of the open well. A tall man with an enormous belly they called "Fats" was working a fiberglass fishing rod back and forth along the water's surface while the others coached and cajoled him. Fats had hooked a four-foot long water moccasin that everyone wanted to see, but nobody wanted up on the deck. After several hectic minutes, Fats cut his line and the angry snake made a lazy lap around the pool with its head just above the water eyeing its tormentors before sinking into the depths from which it had been rudely yanked.

The noise had barely faded away when the owner turned and noticed me standing in the entryway. He jabbed what was left of his pointer finger in my direction and demanded, "What do you want?"

I replied, "My name is Ross Ryan, and I'm here to do a health inspection for the city."

The Angler's Hideaway was owned and operated by Captain Zebulon Cain. Nobody seemed to know what he had ever been a captain of, but everyone called him Cappy.

Cappy was short with a shorter temper, a bronze complexion, matted grey hair, and he wore tan Dickies work pants, which were stained by years of toil and neglect. Cappy's faded plaid shirt had short sleeves and he pulled an unfiltered Camel cigarette from its tattered pocket, lit it with a match and let me know, "I've been running this place for forty years and ain't never had no health inspector come in here. I don't reckon I need one now."

Anticipating a verbal row, the weathered men in the background turned their full attention toward our unprecedented confrontation. I stood my ground, stared into Cappy's yellowed eyes and said, "Well, sir, if you've been forty years without an inspection, I'd say you were way past due."

This brought howls of approval from the gallery, which seemed to mollify Cappy. He dangled his Camel from the side of his mouth Bogart style and thrust his callused hand at my midsection. With ashes falling he said, "Sonny, my name's Cappy and what I say around here goes. You tell me what you got on your mind to do today and I'll tell you if it's going to happen or not."

I said, "Fair enough, Cappy. I plan to inspect your premises and write down anything that is not up to the standards set by the State of Texas Health Department. Then you and I will go over my report and try to figure out a way to bring The Angler's Hideaway up to code."

Cappy scratched his greasy head and belched out blue smoke as he replied, "I reckon you can do what you want for now. I got lunch to make for these boys." With that said, he went into the kitchen and filled two deep fryers with baskets of frozen French fries.

I started poking around the old dining room first. The

vinyl booths were all torn and their Formica tabletops scratched beyond repair. Most of the ancient carpet had been pushed into a roll at one end of the room exposing the water damage from years of roof leaks. It was apparent that the Fish O Rama had not served diners for decades and was now being used for the storage of paper goods, fishing supplies and plastic utensils. The room was dank with cracked windows and peeling paint on the walls.

I walked outside and avoided the grill area while Cappy worked in a cloud of greasy smoke. A row of five small boat slips stretched off the south side of the main building. They were rickety and several of the flotation drums that held them up had rusted through creating a wavy walkway to challenge anyone who dared to land there by boat. Two restrooms on this side of the building buzzed with flies and the water valves to their toilets had to be turned on and off each time they were used to avoid running constantly.

Leading from the north side of the enclosed shelter was a finger of floating pier that reached toward the main body of the lake. A rail of rusty pipe encircled this platform and dozens of rusted metal chairs lined the edge facing open water. At night on weekends and warm holidays this dock would be packed with hefty women in double-knit pants, gorging on salty snacks and gossiping under a sparse row of white street lamps while they fished for bottom feeders.

Cappy was serving the last grilled cheese sandwich of his short lunch rush when I entered the kitchen area. The kitchen equipment was World War II vintage and the damp lake air had rusted everything that wasn't caked in layers of cooking grease.

Only one of the three ancient coolers was holding below the maximum allowable temperature of forty-five degrees. I could see through the wooden floor where water drained directly into the lake from the dish- and hand-washing sinks. The Angler's Hideaway would never be brought up to current code requirements without a total makeover.

I took my many pages of violations to the front counter where Cappy was surveying his domain with an after lunch Camel. He feigned attention as I plodded through my list of shortcomings, which lasted through a second smoke.

When I finished he turned to face me for the first time and said, "Sonny, I'm about to educate you to 'The Grandfather Clause.' Ya see, old-timers like me, who was in business long before them codes you been goin' on about was written don't have to follow the new rules. We are exempt 'cause we been doin' things our way longer than you've been alive. 'The Grandfather Clause' keeps old codgers from going out of business trying to patch things up to make you happy every time you think up a new rule. What do you think about that?"

Every inspector who ever lived knew and dreaded the infamous "Grandfather Clause." Yes, exceptions would always have to be made to avoid creating hardships for older establishments when new rules are written, but the Grandfather Clause was never meant to be a catchall dodge for run-down enterprises. Cappy had played his ace excuse right off the bat and I'd heard it too many times to allow a blanket clemency.

I said, "Cappy, The Angler's Hideaway is what it is and I don't expect you to spruce it up to like-new condition. I do expect you to get rid of things like that roll of rotting carpet in the old dining room and fix boards and railings that somebody might get hurt on when they give way. I also insist that you store perishable foods at the right temperatures and keep your kitchen a heck of a lot cleaner. What do you think about that?"

I wouldn't call it surprise, maybe more of a mild shock that spread over Cappy's craggy face. I waited for the explosion, but all he said was, "That sounds fair enough, I reckon." He picked up my stack of notes and added, "It looks like we got some work to do around here."

I hadn't noticed, but all the old fishermen had stopped what they were doing and focused on Cappy and me when I approached the counter with my report. They seemed thoroughly disappointed when no fight ensued. The general hum of conversation replaced the hush that had taken over the room.

I pointed out the most pressing corrections to be made, like moving meats and other perishable foods into the only working cooler and using the others to store prepackaged foods that weren't temperature sensitive. Cappy agreed to address the blatant problems immediately and said he would work on the repairs as time and money allowed. He was still reading my notes when I walked out into the bright sunshine and across the flooded parking lot.

I returned many times over the years to The Angler's Hideaway and it did improve steadily. It will never be a four-star establishment, but then again the entire clientele would fish somewhere else if that type of drastic transformation were to occur.

Cappy never learned my name and continued to address me as "Sonny" when I made inspection calls. He never failed to invoke the "Grandfather Clause" whenever I pointed out anything that was going to cost him some money to correct, and I never let him get away with it if the rule did not apply. I was sure that Cappy did not like me and I dreaded going to The Angler's Hideaway, but we could work together and that was all that this situation demanded.

I did pay one very unofficial and anonymous visit to The Angler's Hideaway. It was well after midnight with a bulbous full moon overhead and just enough breeze to keep my small sailboat moving steadily, which eased the unbearable swelter of an intense August heat wave. It was a night fraught with boredom-induced mischief fueled by over imbibing producing a complete lack of inhibitions.

I was sailing with my girlfriend, Denise and another couple, Jake and Matty Jean McCrackin. Matty Jean sat forward on the boat's cabin and pointed off into the distance at a row of artificial lights on the far end of the silvery lake. Matty Jean asked in her thick southern drawl, "Ross, what on earth could be open on the lake at this time of night?"

Looking to see what she was referring to I replied, "That's got to be The Angler's Hideaway."

Matty Jean looked confused and asked, "Pray tell, what is an Angler's Hideaway?"

I thought for a minute about how to describe such an establishment and settled on, "It's an old floating dock where people pay to sit and fish. It must be open this late to provide a place for the Hideaway's less than wealthy patrons to escape this oppressive heat."

Matty Jean asked, "Can we sail over there for little look?"

The wind was right for a nice reach to the west and I replied, "I don't see why not."

I tacked the boat toward The Angler's Hideaway and Jake brought up a pair of binoculars from below deck. Jake, Denise and Matty Jean took turns gazing at the people fishing on the

Hideaway's outside deck. Matty Jean commented, "My, aren't they a sturdy bunch of gals? They look like the bean-snappin' ladies who gather to gossip on the farms back home, except they don't appear to be havin' much fun."

As we neared the docks I could see several dozen working class ladies about to doze off as they sat along the water's edge with their long cane poles leaning against the rusty handrail in front of them. I eased the boat off the wind so we could glide past the dock parallel to the sleepy women. The moon created a broad path of silver light from behind us and with no motor running the white boat with white sails would glide into the glare of the overhead lights on the dock before the ladies ever saw or heard us coming.

Less than one hundred yards away Matty Jean turned to me with a devilish twinkle in her eye and said, "Let's all get buck naked and sit as still as statues while we sail by. That ought to liven up those old gals."

Before anyone could answer Matty Jean had shucked her swimsuit and assumed a demure pose in the buff on the cabin top facing the Hideaway. The rest of us followed as instructed and then froze for our debut as we entered the harsh lights. I did not think about all the extended fishing lines until the keel of my boat snagged the first one we sailed over. This brought the fisherwoman cradling the pole to life and the excitement spread as I caught every line along the row on the way by. The women had been suddenly aroused from their sleepy state by the violent jerking of their fishing rods anticipating the rewards of catching a huge fish only to see a ghost ship with four nude models drift past them and fade into the night.

We continued to hear the sounds of raucous laughter,

shouting and excited ranting for several miles across the placid water as we sailed away from The Fisherman's Hideaway. Matty Jean looked ever so pleased with herself and said: "I just knew those gals could use a little lift tonight. I believe we've given them plenty to talk about."

Indeed we had. I heard infinite versions of the mysterious ghost ship with a naked crew for years to come upon subsequent inspections at The Angler's Hideaway. It had been a once in a lifetime event, but the taletellers were all in agreement that one day the mystery boat would return. I'm sure this provided endless hours of speculation when things got slow at night while fishing on the rundown docks.

Armies of inspectors were unleashed from the upper level each day to insure that water lines, streets, buildings, violation corrections and property improvements were carried out according to code in proper Bliss fashion.

CHAPTER 15
THE CODE OF THE WEST

Dick Darling wasted no time initiating the build up of Bliss's city government and setting into motion the construction of a spanking new Civic Center to house his burgeoning creation. Layers of management were created to insulate Dick from the demanding citizenry and provide lesser fish to throw to the sharks when things went wrong. Dick allowed the existing department heads to believe they were all in the running for the new mid-level management positions and the resulting head butting got ugly at times.

A restructuring of the ranks was also on Dick's agenda and every department head feared losing control of his or her domain. A power grab ensued and Rex Flint threw himself headlong into the fray. Unfortunately, Rex did not see the advantage of getting rid of the division's most obnoxious duties and assignments during the realignment, but others did.

A wise old owl named Gene Autrey ran the Building Inspection Division. Gene was forever explaining how his name was spelled with an "e" and he was not related in any way to the "Singing Cowboy." Gene seemed to have been on hand when the first dirt clod was turned for construction in Bliss and I learned a lot from his easy going but firm demeanor.

Gene deftly unloaded the inspections of new signs and fences from his division and they landed squarely on Rex. Along with the added duties, two of Gene's long time employees crossed over to the ranks of the newly created Health and Code Enforcement Division. Ms. Lily Samone and Ms. Tara Hanks moved into the tiny red jail and we were suddenly bursting at the seams.

Ms. Lily once told me she had three birth control babies: one while on the pill, one while fitted with an IUD and a condom child. Ms. Lily had been through several husbands along the way but currently was unattached. Ms. Lily shot straight from the hip, refrained from anything that could be construed as delicate talk, and I appreciated her candor, but I made it a point to avoid her wrath.

Ms. Tara had been through a husband or two as well. Ms. Tara loved to dance and frequented the local boot-scootin' honky-tonks looking for the perfect cowboy. Lord knows there has never been a perfect cowboy, and I'm afraid her quest was doomed to be perpetual from the start.

Bruce, Jocko and I were quick to dump as much of our code enforcement duties on the new arrivals as we thought they could stand without going stark raving gooney. The newness of it all overwhelmed them and they were thrust into the thick of things with the slightest amount of training and instruction, just as the rest of us had been. Welcome aboard, ladies.

By the time that our cramped quarters in the old jail had caused us to want to strangle each other, the news came down from on high that we would be moving to the new Civic Center. Most of us had never been inside the new building as inspections of the facility had been kept to a bare minimum to keep construction moving at a brisk pace. You can't fight city hall, especially while it's under construction.

The excitement of moving into a shiny new building wore off rather quickly as we were introduced to our new working environment. Those of us who had previously worked from our own offices, however small and cramped, suddenly found ourselves elbow to elbow in open rows of four surrounded only by file cabinets at every second row. We soon learned that all conversations and phone calls would be shared with the entire floor. To ease our pain department heads and their assistants were given offices with doors and windows along the length of one side of our busy room. Bitterness abounded.

Under the new regime, the entire second floor of the Bliss Civic Center was occupied by the newly created Community Development Department. Offices for Engineers, building inspectors, health and code inspectors, fire inspectors, community planners and zoning experts were all housed here. Pretty much everyone who played a part in building and maintaining private properties in the city landed on the second floor.

A firebrand from the Fire Prevention Division had been anointed to run Community Development much to the dismay of the other department heads. He was a bowling ball of a man named Barney Belcher, who constantly spewed malapropisms and had the demeanor of a used car salesman. Barney could tick off the Pope one minute and sell him a new miter the next. Barney had been around as long as Gene Autrey and was the perfect punching bag for the public's wrath when they were introduced to Dick's new permits and user fees.

The central scrutinizer, Dick Darling, sat at the rear entrance on the first floor of the new Civic Center and had his own escape exit to the outside. The bean counters, tax masters, record keepers, personnel people, and assorted administrative staff were all cloistered in lower level offices. White-collar wonks from the first floor rarely ventured up to the what they considered the zoo operating above them, but we wandered freely among first floor types gathering information about citizens and property for reports and violation letters.

Indeed the second floor was a nonstop circus. Armies of inspectors were unleashed from the upper level each day to insure that water lines, streets, buildings, violation corrections and property improvements were carried out according to code in proper Bliss fashion. The bedraggled bunch returned around noon to check in before lunch and then they were off again until the evening business hours. A flurry of angry, confused or just plain argumentative phone calls would pour in from the Bliss citizenry for inspectors to sort out, appease or clarify the demands they had placed on unwitting souls while performing their civic duties.

Dozens of fever pitch phone calls welled up during the final working countdown as last minute pleas were made for lenience, extensions or exceptions to the rules by contractors, violators and developers who felt persecuted. The public servant's song and dance would be initiated in every case to cajole the caller into doing the right thing, while being ever so careful not to upset them to the point of escalating their issues to a higher authority.

Failure to placate an angry constituent could result in the

worst possible outcome, a fiery letter addressed to the City Manager. A single letter of alleged maltreatment to Dick Darling would send a shock wave of overreaction throughout Community Development as accused abusers scrambled to justify their actions with detailed reports and records of the steps they'd taken to handle the situation. Woe to the poor inspectors who haphazardly documented their calls and communications with irate complainants. Dick immediately viewed all city employees as guilty until they could extricate themselves from the public stew and no help from supervisors or division heads could be expected, as they were busy ducking and covering to avoid any of the fan flung flack from landing on them.

A constant parade of contractors in muddy boots, developers in shiny suits and local yokels with rolls of hand-sketched plans marched their way to the upper deck to seek approval and permits for their schemes and projects. Plans were submitted for review and money changed hands when all the division heads signed off on a proposal. It could take weeks or minutes, depending on the complexity of the work to be undertaken, and every propounder wanted his deal done yesterday.

In an effort to cut back on the amount of preposterous plans submitted that could never come close to meeting Bliss's code requirements, Wednesdays were set aside for any and everyone with an idea to take a free shot at getting Community Development to buy off on their dream without going through formal channels and paying fees.

Thirty minutes were allotted for the proponent's dog and pony show with a representative from each department at the table. These meetings were devised to handle the rush of local property owners who were anxious to cash in on Bliss's unbridled growth, but not willing to pay a professional planner to work on their idea until they were sure it was feasible. It did not take long for the real players in the development game to start taking advantage of these free consultations and the agendas could alternate from the serious to the absurd every half-hour.

Barney Belcher presided over Wednesday's plan gatherings in a large room he also used for staff meetings. Normally Rex would represent the Health and Code Department, but when he was incapacitated by chronic sinus failure or the myriad of other manifestations resulting from his hypochondria, one of his health inspectors would be dispatched to substitute. Jocko would be next in line, but he was busy soothing a family whose dog had been gunned down by an over-achieving Animal Control officer, so I was drafted to attend my first Wednesday planning session.

I walked across the hall and entered the meeting room early to locate my seat, so as not to sit in someone else's favorite spot and rumple any inflated ego feathers. There sat Barney at the head of a huge table presiding over an impromptu department head meeting. India born and educated, Kaushal Vikramendra or Vik for short, sat on Barney's left. Vik was our quiet and kind city engineer, but pronounced his "V's" as "W's," which never failed to crack me up. Gene Autrey was at the other end of the table and another Bliss lifer, George Lumpkin from Planning and Zoning, came in when I did from a door at the opposite end of the room. Barney's right-hand man and heir apparent to the Community Development throne, Red Ferrel, was currently the Bliss Fire Marshal and he laughed out loud at the surprised look on my face when I froze in the doorway.

Barney pointed at a chair that Gene was rolling away from the table and said, "Come on in and sit down. We're done with this shindig anyway. Gene show Ryan the list and try and keep him out of trouble when the next show starts."

I sat down and Gene handed me a copy of the day's appointments. I was thankful that only the first two time slots were filled.

Gene leaned toward me and said, "Don't worry too much. This is pretty informal and if you don't have a hundred percent sure answer for a question, just tell them you'll research it and get back to them as soon as possible. That's what Rex does."

At exactly one o'clock four men in suits that cost more than my yearly salary filed into the room and took the vacant seats along one side of the table. They were the advance engineering team for a giant mall that was going to go up on the old Ruselow Ranch. One of the men never took off his designer sunglasses and occasionally whispered into a cell phone during the meeting.

These guys rolled out a log-sized set of plans detailing the streets, water lines and sewer criteria for their fast approaching development. Vik and Red hunched over the pile of curly papers leaving the rest of us to sit back and watch while they argued over the size of pipes and distance to fire hydrants Bliss would require them to install. It was intensely boring until Vik took off on revisions that he deemed necessary on a new street to be named Valley View at its intersection with Vista View.

Vik said, "Gentlemen these Walley Woo waste water lines won't work.

Cool Shades stopped whispering into his phone long enough to look up and ask, "Why?"

Vik went on, "We're planning a new waste water substation on Wista Woo that requires wider water line easements to separate the potable water from the waste water."

Cool Shades smirks at Vik and says, "Oh, really?"

Vik was cool, but I could tell he didn't like the man in the designer sunglasses. The other three engineers were eager to get revisions without upsetting Vik, who they knew would ultimately approve their final drawings. Barney was busy cleaning his fingernails with a small pocketknife and let the scene play itself out.

Cool Shades says to Vik, "And when did you plan on letting us in on this new substation?"

The air would have been very tense if we weren't all holding in gut-busting laughter after Vik's first round of flying "W's." George answered Cool Shades, "That substation has been on the books for years," but you could tell he was on the verge of losing it when he gave the reply.

Cool Shades sat up straight and clenched his cell phone in a tight fist. It was impossible to tell if he was glaring through those dark glasses when he asked George, "Do you think this is funny?"

George said, "Not at all."

Vik went to a dry-erase board behind Barney to illustrate his point. As he drew he explained, "Right here where Walley Woo and Wista Woo cross, the walkways will have to move west so the waste water lines will remain uncovered. The water lines were here, but if you move them to Walley Woo instead, no widening of the easement will be warranted."

I glanced at Gene and he whispered, "It doesn't get any better than that."

The bustle of the three attentive engineers rolling up their plans and thanking Vic as they attempted to hustle Cool Shades out of the meeting covered my stifled giggles. I turned away from their exodus to keep from making anyone think I was amused by their problem. Junior Jones slipped into the room as the engineers squeezed out and was sitting directly across from me when I regained my composure and turned around.

A Mr. Jones had been listed on our short agenda for one-thirty, but I never equated the name with Junior. He was there to present his plan for Junior's Jump n Jive. He gave me a scowl and turned toward Barney to say, "How's it goin'?"

Barney and Junior had been hunting buds before Junior's property got annexed into the Bliss city limits and he became a royal pain in the backside for everyone in Community Development. After Junior's catfish farm dried up and his landfill got nixed we were ready for just about anything he could conjure up. Barney rolled his eyes and asked, "What you got for us today, Junior?" I didn't know it, but Junior had become a Wednesday meeting regular.

Junior pulled out a twelve-pack beer carton that had been opened up so he could draw his plans on the unadorned inside. A vague outline of Junior's property could be discerned with a dozen small squares bunched together at one end surrounded by a fence. An entry drive with a small parking lot and a tiny building were sketched near the State Road. Junior slid his creation across the table toward Barney with a big smile.

Barney furrowed his brows, took one glance and asked, "What the hell is that supposed to be?"

Junior bit his lip and replied, "It's a trampoline park. I'm gonna call it Junior's Jump n Jive."

This revelation brought the house down. There was very little professional decorum in Junior's presentation and none was being offered in return. Gene said, "Junior, you've outdone yourself on this one."

Junior looked hurt and began to explain, "No, really. Ya see I can get a deal on these trampolines that go over a hole in the ground so when someone falls off they don't have that far to drop. All I need is a little shack to collect money and a gravel parking lot. I'm gonna rent these things by the hour to people who are afraid their kids might fall off one of them trampolines way up in the air on a frame."

Barney grinned and said, "Junior, are you sure you ain't gone and fell off one of them trampazeens yourself?

The color drained from Junior's face and Red picked up the ball, "Junior, you're going to have to have a paved parking lot that can support a fire engine and a painted fire lane. On the bright side, the hydrant that the church put in next to your place will cover you."

Gene added, "Your shack will have to have a public restroom and meet the current building codes for water and electric. I hope you plan on charging a lot of money for them bouncing customers."

George said, "I'm not sure what the proper zoning for a trampoline facility is, but I'll research it and get back to you."

I never added a word. I had been the bearer of Junior's bad news too many times and I knew there would come another day when we would be at odds. Junior picked up his beer carton, folded it in half and left in a huff.

Barney called it a short Wednesday and dismissed us all from his presence. Everybody gathered up their code and ordinance books and returned to their offices. It was just another day of trampled dreams on the second floor of the Bliss Civic Center.

But that ain't no swimmin' pool. I've been growing me some monster bass in there. Fish is the only things swimmin' in that pool.

CHAPTER 16
SWIMMING POOLS

In the mad scramble to justify our meager Health Department salaries and increase revenue, it was noted that the city of Bliss did not require permits and regular inspections of its many semi-public pools. Including apartments, condos, schools and day care facilities Bliss had about seventy-five swimming pools and hot tubs that could be charged a permit fee for monthly inspections during the summer swimming season.

I was selected to attend a two-day training class provided by the State Health Department to obtain instruction on how to properly maintain pools. A thorough analysis was given on the reactions of pool chemicals used to achieve a specified acceptable water quality. Several complicated explanations were proffered regarding the detrimental effects of sunlight, temperature and pool loads as related to the size, depth and volume of each individual pool's water capacity. I then endured a lengthy dissertation on the inner workings of pool filters, passed an exam and became the pool expert for the Bliss Health Department. I was even awarded a little certificate proclaiming me capable of teaching others the magic of performing proper pool maintenance.

What I quickly learned in the field was that if you checked the chemicals every day, balanced the pH, removed debris from the water and cleaned the filters ninety-nine percent of all pools would be just fine. Since apartment maintenance men, with more pressing problems like plumbing leaks, broken air conditioners and building repairs, were usually assigned the pool chores as an afterthought they welcomed my simplistic approach to keeping their pools open. The more sun and the more people your pool comes in contact with the more chlorine it will need. Acid makes the pH go down and soda ash makes it go up; just remember to experiment with small doses to avoid the dreaded pH bounce. That's all there is to it.

I would attempt to inspect as many pools as possible in the early morning hours before the temperatures reached triple digits and the relentless Texas sun began scorching everything it shined upon. Pretty people that worked as bartenders, wait persons and entertainers at night could be found tanning at adult only complexes in the late morning hours, and I adjusted my inspection schedule and route accordingly.

Most pools were crowded with screaming children home on their summer vacations. Tired mothers lounged around the pools pretending to watch them. I became an instant target for splashes from cannonballs and preacher's seats whenever I knelt at the edge of child infested waters to draw samples for testing. Getting wet on a blistering summer day was not a hardship, but water spoiled my paperwork and I found out that the ink from certain pens ran like a river when wet. If a mother did intervene on my behalf to stop the splashing onslaught, several children would gather around me and strike up a continuous question session about what I was doing and why. Nobody is safe from bored children.

Having your pool closed was an unforgivable sin for any maintenance person. The usual culprit was a low chlorine count. Heat and sunlight can destroy chlorine concentrations and dirty people will cause it to quickly burn away. A dog in the pool can do the damage of fifty filthy people. Kicking a pool full of angry mothers and children out of the water on a red-hot day creates an irate mob capable of lynching. With suddenly no place to go but back to a small apartment and nothing to do when they get there, the situation is downright dangerous.

The hapless maintenance person will immediately add the missing chlorine, but it can take hours for the concentrated granules to disperse and bring the water up to the required level. Having been locked out of the fenced pool enclosure, the seething crowd will descend upon the apartment offices and a bewildered and overwhelmed manager will set off the maintenance person's beeper while he is working to correct the problem.

The desperate maintenance worker will begin begging me to come back as soon as possible to reopen his pool. If I manage to return later in the day and find the pool ready to reopen, the grateful maintenance person will have become my friend for life.

I was able to inspect all my pools at least once each month the first summer. Then the apartment building boom took off at an alarming rate and I quickly became swamped. Jocko and Bruce were drafted to help out and I was supposed to train them. Bruce was no problem, but Jocko was on one of his body bulking binges and highly susceptible to heat. Just kneeling to scoop up a water sample had left Jocko sweating profusely and swaying with a vacant look on his ashen face in the late morning sun by the pool's edge during our first outing. I contemplated letting him fall to see if he would go into the pool or crash on the concrete deck, but I thought better of it and steered him into the shade where he settled into a plastic chair that bent with his weight. When he came around we decided that he should only inspect pools in the cool of the morning.

We only inspected private pools in people's back yards when the neighbors would call and rat them out. Peering over a wooden fence or down from a second floor next door, the complainant would note that the owner had let his pool turn green or brown and call the Health Department to force him to get it back to sparkling clear.

Responding to just such a complaint, I was peering over a six-foot wooden fence at a pool that had achieved swamp-like qualities. A huge man, wearing only cut-off shorts, came bounding through a sliding glass door into the back yard to confront me. He ran right at me shouting, "Who the hell do you think you're spying on, pervert?"

Startled, I lost my footing on the bottom cross member of the fence and slipped out of sight behind it. When I looked up the burly man's head was staring over the fence and down at me. He showered me with saliva yelling, "You can just get your sorry butt out of here before I come across this fence and give it a good thrashin'!"

I reached into my pocket, pulled out my badge and shined it up into his eyes. I said, "That won't be necessary, I'm with the Bliss Health Department and I was just checking out a complaint on your pool. According to the tax records, you must be Mr. Spivey."

Mr. Spivey replied, "Well, I'll be. Why didn't you just come around the front and knock on the door then?"

I shrugged and said, "These complaints aren't always legitimate and I figured I would verify that we had a problem before involving you. Sometimes after a quick look I can chalk up a complaint to an angry neighbor and go on my way."

Mr. Spivey demanded, "Who in hell turned me in and for what?"

I told him, "The complaint was made anonymously and the problem is with your swimming pool."

Mr. Spivey shot back, "I ain't got no problem with the pool and you can come in here and see for yourself."

Mr. Spivey opened the alley gate and I went into his back yard. The pool looked worse from close up. There were aquatic plants growing in the murky water and bubbles rising at one end. I said, "Mr. Spivey…"

He stopped me and said, "Hell, just call me Moose.

I went on, "OK, Moose. The Bliss pool ordinance says that the water in your swimming pool has to be clear enough to see the bottom at all times. If somebody were to fall into your pool now, nobody could see to save them."

Moose scratched his head and replied, "But that ain't no swimmin' pool. I've been growing me some monster bass in there. Fish is the only things swimmin' in that pool." To illustrate his point, Moose grabbed a handful of fish pellets from a tin under a table near the pool and tossed them into the water. The water's surface boiled with fish activity.

It was my turn to say, "Well, I'll be."

Moose went on, "I got me one of them bubble makers, like's in the live well of a bass boat only bigger, goin' down there in the deep end. Ever time I catch me a real lunker, I bring it home and toss it in. I figure to breed me some super bass and then put 'em back into my favorite honey holes."

I didn't reply right away. With a look of concern I said, "But that's still a swimming pool and according to the ordinance you are in violation."

Moose shot back, "How's this any different than them ponds where rich folks grow them giant Jappo goldfish in their back yards? There ain't no skeeters in there, cause the fish eat 'em and I don't see how I'm a hurtin' a soul."

I asked, "You mean a Coy Pond?"

Moose replied, "Yup, them's the ones."

I said, "I don't know. Moose, I'm going to have to do some research on this one. You're my first outdoor bass aquarium."

Moose said, "You just go ahead on and let me know what you find out. I sure would hate to lose my bass."

I called The State Health Department and mulled the problem over with Rex and the rest of our group. I sort of wanted Moose to be able to keep his prized fish, but the final decision did not go his way. It was deemed that even Coy Ponds have to remain clear enough to see the bottom in the event that a child fell in and required rescuing. Also, Moose's pool was much deeper and posed a larger threat than any shallow Coy Pond.

I called Moose and he answered on the fist ring, "Howdy!"

I replied, "Moose, this is Ross Ryan at the Health Department."

Moose said, "Hey, Ross, how's it hangin'?"

I laughed and said, "Good, thank you. I'm calling about your bass pond. I'm afraid you're going to have to clean that thing up and turn it back into a swimming pool."

Moose laughed hard and said, "Well that's just fine, I figured them college boys was goin' to go agin me so I done took my bass to my favorite fishin' spots and turned 'em out. Besides, my wife was startin' to have fits about the pool anyway. I'll get it cleaned up in short order."

I said, "Thanks, Moose. I appreciate you working with me on this problem."

Just before Moose hung up he added, "Just don't come snoopin' around here and peekin' over my fences anymore if you have a bone to pick with me. Go ahead and come on 'round to the front door and let's settle it like men. Besides, you ain't such a bad guy for the law."

I assured him that I would confront him personally with any future complaints. Moose did return his pool water to human swimming quality, and I satisfied another customer.

My fight or flight mechanism went on the fritz and I froze in place. He walked toward me with the huge hammer dangling from his right hand.

CHAPTER 17

FENCES

Not long after Moose and I became best buds some kid managed to climb over a fence in a nearby town and drown himself. It was an awful tragedy and the child's parents sued the pool's owner and the tiny town for negligence and won a pot of money. It was deemed in court that the town should have had a fence ordinance that detailed the construction and requirements for fences surrounding swimming pools and the owner should have been more vigilant in keeping the neighbor kids out of his back yard.

When I was a child growing up I detested those parables that always started out, "Why when I was a kid…" but doggone it somewhere along the way parents quit being responsible for their children and started pointing fingers at anyone but themselves when one of their little angels did something wrong. If I had climbed over somebody's six-foot wooden fence and got caught trespassing, my parents would not have been angry with the property owner; they would have straightened me out in short order for being where I didn't belong. Now days we are all responsible for everybody else's children.

Bliss officials reacted to the swimming pool catastrophe in typical knee-jerk fashion by decreeing that a new fence ordinance be written. Underlying the sudden concern about child safety and the possibility of being sued was the opportunity to slap a hefty permit fee on every new fence that was being built in Bliss. With the pace of new housing construction at an all-time high, fences were springing up by the hundreds and the city's cash register would soon have another cause for ringing.

Naturally, since I had just attended a two-day pool school and a swimming pool accident had triggered the rush for a new ordinance, I was selected to draft the fence law. I had never written an ordinance. I did know that there was no such thing as a perfect ordinance that covers every imaginable and unforeseeable condition and that people are trying to figure out a way to get around any new ordinance long before it can be completed and adopted by a governing body.

My instructions were to call every city, town and hamlet within one hundred miles and have them send me a copy of their fence ordinance. It's called, "Not reinventing the wheel" and I don't know how the writer of the first-ever fence ordinance got started. Next I contacted county, state and federal entities that dealt with fence requirements for their input. I ended up with a stack of reading material you could hide behind.

I attempted to cull the most sensible requirements from my heap of information and incorporate them into my new directive. I kept all the original distance setbacks for easements and visibility to avoid performing traffic studies to justify new ones. When I finished, my new ordinance didn't look terribly different from the old one, except for some hefty increases in permit and inspection fees.

I did beef-up the requirements for fences around swimming pools and gave them their own little section. Those cross supports, like the one I was standing on when I met Moose, would now have to be on the inside of wooden fences surrounding home pools to keep kids from using them to shinny over. The gates would have to be self-closing and self-latching. Building garbage can holders or stacking things like wood along the outside of a pool's fence was also prohibited to thwart climbers.

I took my masterpiece to the city attorney's office for Sheila Swift to give it her legal blessing, and it came back with more red ink than our federal budget. Common sense does not an ordinance make; and I had failed to point out obvious things like six-foot wooden fences in the city could not be built around front yards, and houses could not be made impregnable to emergency and utility responders. I had failed to address subdivision covenants, government property exclusions and maintenance. The list went on and additions were made with each subsequent submittal until we created a hefty tome.

As the author of the new fence legislation my presence was required when the lengthy document was submitted to the Bliss City Council for approval. It was Barney Belcher's job to sit on the front row with all the other department heads and answer council members' questions, but he loved to turn with a sweep of his arm and summon a lackey for any explanations that might contain complications. The council gave the new ordinance a cursory thumbing-through and passed it with little argument as they did with anything that appeared arduous or they thought they might not easily grasp.

Housing contractors liked to play a little game with the city when obtaining fence permits. To maintain the frantic pace at which new subdivisions were sprouting in every vacant field in Bliss, they would instruct their fence building subcontractors to install their fences without a permit and gamble on getting things right. Contractors would then submit thirty to fifty fence permit applications at one time and an overloaded inspector would often find the fences completed when he checked on the site to approve the permits.

This worked in everybody's favor when the fences met all the code requirements. The inspector could approve the permit and sign off on the final product in one trip. But when the fence was found to be in violation and needed adjustment, it was the subcontractor that got left holding the bag.

I was working my way down a nail-strewn alley with a pile of fence permit applications in one hand and a tape measure in the other. It was after four-thirty and the normal cacophony of hammering, shouting, power saws and heavy equipment had died down for the day. I was inspecting eight-foot fences that smelled of freshly sawn wood. The pine slats still oozed sap where they had been nailed to their cross braces. In the distance around a gentle curve in the alley I could hear the sound of one air-driven staple gun tacking boards together and the hum of its compressor at work.

My inspection was not going well. Every fence in a row of ten along the west side of the pavement had been set two-feet too close to the alley. The entire row would have to be uprooted and moved back to meet the setback requirement.

I rounded the bend to inspect the last fence and there stood the fence builder I'd heard working earlier loading equipment into his truck. I measured the fence he'd just completed and noted my rejection on the permit application for failing to meet the setback requirement.

The fence builder approached me and asked, "Who are you?

I replied, "I'm Ross Ryan and I'm with the Bliss Department of Health and Code Enforcement."

Before I could continue he demanded, "What's that got to do with my fences?"

I showed him the permit applications and said, "I'm here to inspect these lots for approval of these fence permit applications."

He looked incredibly confused and pointed out that, "These fences are already built."

It was a brilliant deduction. I replied, "Yes, but do you have a permit for them?"

He said, "No, I'm just the sub. The general contractor pulls all the permits."

I knew it was about to get awkward. In an even and inoffensive tone I explained, "What I have in my hand are the contractor's fence permit applications. What has occurred here is that he's had you build these fences before I could come to the site and approve his submitted plans. It happens all the time. The problem is that every fence on this side of the alley will have to be moved back two feet"

The fence builder said, "You're kidding me, right?"

I shook my head and said, "I'm afraid not."

The fence builder was a young strapping lad with a deep tan.

His face slowly grew redder until crimson displaced the bronze as the impact of what I said began to settle in on him. He turned and strode in measured steps to the back of his truck where he pulled out a ten-pound sledgehammer with a long handle. My fight or flight mechanism went on the fritz and I froze in place. He walked toward me with the huge hammer dangling from his right hand. He raised the hammer high above his head, walked right past me and began a savage attack on the fence. Wood splintered and took flight in all directions. Support posts were knocked from their concrete footings with two whacks and he downed a fifty-foot section of fence in less than ten minutes. It was a magnificent display of destruction.

He turned in a rage at the end of the row and screamed at me, "There! Are you happy now?"

I yelled back, "I am not the problem here!"

The fence builder slumped in exhaustion. He trudged back toward me and was a sweaty mess when he put his hammer back in the truck. He turned to face me again and said, "Man, I'm sorry. I've got a bit of temper."

I sure as heck didn't want to set him off again, so I refrained from the obvious comeback and said, "If I were you, I'd take the rest of the fences down a little slower so you can reuse most of the material. In the future you might want to wait until you have an approved permit in your hand before you put a fence up. I think I would also try and make your contractor cough up some extra bucks for correcting these fences."

The fence builder just nodded his head yes. He was spent. He was still standing and staring at the fence row when I walked away.

Contractors continued to play the build now and hope for the best game with fence permits and most of the time the results were worth the gamble. I ran into several more strings of misplaced fence rows that required relocating, but I never witnessed another show like the young fence builder put on that day with his sledgehammer. I hope I never do.

It was as if I was witnessing the Five Chinese Stooges at work in some Asian television studio.

CHAPTER 18
THE MALL

The Horizon Hills Mall sprawled across a complete section on the west end of the Ruselow Ranch where two state highways crossed the north to south Interstate and the new by-pass would someday dead-end. It provided a state of the art shopping experience with all the big retailers like Spears, Willards, J. C. Cents, and Bloomingsales anchoring the mall's corners from day one. While the mall itself continued to grow over the years, clusters of retail shops, strip centers, stand alone stores and restaurants fought for space with apartment and condominium complexes in the adjacent fields. The gentle rolling grasslands of the Ruselow Ranch were transformed into an expansive cityscape.

There was no weeping or gnashing of teeth over the loss of pristine prairie because people were getting rich. Not only the Ruselows, but developers, designers, engineers and the City of Bliss were raking in the dough. Bliss had unleashed a cash cow that supplied a continuous source of revenue from taxes, permit fees and inspection fees. Horizon Hills Mall put Bliss on the map.

People must get ravenously hungry when they shop. That would explain why the mall's food court contained twenty tiny eating establishments that offered every kind of cuisine required for shoppers to keep up their strength while unburdening themselves of their hard earned cash and toting around big bags of newly acquired treasures. The mall also contained three full-blown restaurants when shopping just became too much and a good rest and big meal were in order to survive.

Food court eateries always had cutesy names like; Wally's Wieners, Jo Mama's Pizza, Krazy Kreamery, Pete's Eats and The Kooky Cookie. Whether they served chicken chunks or burritos as big as your head, they were always staffed by ill-mannered teenagers working for minimum wage trying desperately not to be seen by their mall-trolling buddies and seem uncool. Occasionally a mom and pop shop would crop up, but the staggering overhead would usually kill their family dream of selling her magic pastries or his mystic bar-b-q and their space would give way to yet another national franchise.

The mall's food court was an all day job for a Health Inspector. The element of surprise would be quickly lost, as word of the inspector's arrival would spread like plague to all the food court's denizens within minutes. This was not a bad thing, as the idea was to get everyone cleaned up and into compliance, which they would be feverishly trying to accomplish as the inspector worked his way from shop to shop.

I always attempted to tackle the worst of the food court's offenders first. Marginal infractions were to be expected and if they were corrected before I saw them in the adjacent eateries it would save the overworked managers who ran them and me a ton of time.

Severe violations that could cause sickness or death were my main concern.

Ping Pow served up authentic Chinese food from a long steam table that separated the kitchen from hungry shoppers who drooled over the heaps of rice and stir-fried concoctions on display. It was not by chance that a solid wall with one swinging door and no windows kept potential customers from witnessing the chaotic frenzy that played out daily during the preparation of Ping Pow's chow.

I was walking down the grease stained corridor that led to the back doors of all the food court's establishments early one morning on my way to inspect Ping Pow. The rotund Greek, that made gyros from slices he carved off of a giant hunk of mystery meat on a rotating spit in his shop, spotted me as I knocked on Ping Pow's rear entry and hurried into his suite to sound the alarm that I was in the building.

A short man with flour on his hands and in his hair opened the back door and asked me something in Mandarin. I held up my health inspector's badge and he retreated into the kitchen with his hands waving in the air while yelling the same six syllables over and over again. Four more Chinese men broke from their huddle around a small black and white television, crushed their cigarettes out on the kitchen floor and flew into a flurry of cooking related activities. It would be another hour before Ping Pow opened, but they were working like there was not a minute to spare.

I asked the group of men loudly, "Who is in charge here?" Not one of them looked up from his self-consuming tasks and I assumed that they could not speak English. It was not uncommon for the food service industries' grunts to arrive long before their managers and begin prepping for the day. I decided to begin my inspection and hope that someone I could converse with would show up by the time I finished.

I can only describe these Chinese men's actions as a comedy of errors. I would have been appalled at their complete lack of proper food service knowledge if their preparations had not been so blatantly bad. It was as if I was witnessing the Five Chinese Stooges at work in some Asian television studio. I wished for English subtitles to explain what they were saying to each other. They worked together as a team, but a really awful team.

Two of the men fired up the giant woks under the greasy vent hood at the far end of the kitchen, but they never bothered to activate the system's exhaust fans. The small space began to quickly fill up with blue smoke, and I turned the fans on just before the smoke detectors summoned emergency personnel. They both bowed to me in thanks.

The flour-covered man that had let me in stood on a plastic milk crate by a grimy prep table in the center of the room. A man with disturbingly thick glasses was busy piling raw chickens from the walk-in cooler on a stained piece of cardboard on the floor by the flour man's feet. A man with a huge cleaver began whacking the chickens into tiny chunks at the end of the prep table before tossing them into a pile. The flour man was retrieving them from the slimy heap for breading. A fine cloud of flour dust began to fill the air.

The two wok men hoisted a huge kettle onto an empty burner and filled it with water. They attempted to pour rice into the cauldron directly from a twenty-five-pound sack but spilled over a pound on the floor around the stove. The wayward rice was scooped up by hand and returned to the bulk rice sack.

Chicken piling man was now stacking raw shrimp and beef cubes in mounds on a rolling cart, which he wheeled into position next to the scalding woks. He placed two five-gallon plastic buckets of mixed vegetables on the floor by the cart and the stir-fry cooks nodded approval in unison. Both cooks threw flash grease on their respective woks and roaring flames leapt into the vent hood's filters. They tossed handfuls of meat and vegetables into their woks and began whipping them around with a vengeance. I had yet to see anybody wash their hands and I had no idea what the Mandarin words for hair restraints might be.

The kitchen's light switches, door knobs, bulk containers, drawer pulls and every other surface touched by human hands were caked with grease, flour and food particles. The floor was becoming more slippery by the minute and the giant cleaver man would rip a piece of cardboard from a growing pile of boxes waiting to be taken to the trash by the back door and place it over particularly slick spots when the going got too dangerous.

It was getting close to opening time and still no owner or manager had arrived. I left the kitchen through the door leading out front behind the steam table. The steam table's wells were full of rusty water and had bits of sour pork and rice floating in them. The storage area under the table was strewn with piles of foam containers and plastic utensils with no protection from the elements. The table's heat units should have been switched on an hour ago to bring it up to the required holding temperature.

It was now minutes to opening. I had several pages of violations and was trying to figure out how to tell the Stooges in the kitchen that they would not be serving the food I'd seen them abusing when a slightly built young girl with raven hair and long red nails jumped over the counter from the mall side and went straight to the cash register. She opened the till with a key that hung around her neck and turned on the steam table's heat elements. I stood in disbelief as she walked past me a second time as if I was not there, sat on a stool by the register, put on her Walkman's headphones and began reading a college history book.

I took two steps and stood in front of her. She peered up from her book with a vacant look and was about to return to her studies when I asked, "Are you the manager?"

She looked up at me again and said, "No." Then she went back to her reading.

The second time I addressed her in a much firmer and louder voice, "We need to talk, now! I am the health inspector and you are not going to open today! Do you understand what I'm saying?"

My forceful declaration finally seemed to get her attention. She removed her headphones and said, "I know you health inspector. It say so on your hat. What you mean we no open?"

I explained, "I've been here for over an hour. Your kitchen employees' food preparation techniques and sanitary practices scare the heck out of me. There is no way I can let you serve what they've been cooking back there."

The girl knitted her brows and said, "Oooo, Ms. Chen no like that at all."

I asked, "Is Ms. Chen the owner or manager, because I need to speak with her as soon as possible."

The girl replied, "Ms. Chen owner, but she no like coming here early. What they do back there that so bad we no open?"

I showed her the five pages of violations I'd been compiling. She sucked air through her clenched teeth and said, "I can't believe they so stupid! I call Ms. Chen now, but she be very angry." The girl made a call on a cell phone she pulled from her pocket and there was a lot of high-pitched screeching involved. She just listened for several minutes before hanging up.

I said, "Do you speak Chinese? I could use your help getting those guys to start cleaning up back there while we wait for Ms. Chen."

She smiled and replied, "Sure. I tell those idiots what to do."

We both walked into the kitchen and things had only gotten worse. The girl looked hard at the five men who were all stirring away and sloshing food out of cooking containers on the stove. She turned a blank stare back at me, glared hard into my eyes and asked, "Who are those guys?"

I said, "What do you mean, who are those guys?"

She said, "I never see these men before in my life!"

I laughed out loud. I just couldn't help it. I told the girl, "Why don't you ask them who they are and why they are here?"

There was a lengthy chat in Chinese between the confused cashier and the Five Stooges. When it was over she turned to me and said, "They friends of the regular cooks who work here. They all live together. Our cooks are sick today, so they come in to work in their place."

Before I could answer the back door burst open and in flew Ms. Chen. She took a quick glance around the kitchen and burst into a Chinese rant. She was yelling at the cashier and then she pointed and shouted at the cooks. I just stood and waited for her to wear herself down. She ended her little tirade after a heated exchange that was very one-sided with the cashier.

Ms. Chen then seemed to try and compose herself before

turning to me and asking, "What we need to do to open today?"

I said, "All the food they've prepared so far will have to be thrown-out."

Ms. Chen yelled, "All of it?"

I replied, "Yes, all of it. They will have to clean this place up and start over."

Ms. Chen's face was crimson. She said, "It too late to start over. Lunch rush start soon."

I pointed at my paperwork and said, "I am closing your store until all of these items are corrected and..."

Ms. Chen stopped me in mid-sentence, "You can't close me! I lose too much money."

I held my hand up to stop her and got dead serious. Speaking in low even tones I said, "Ms. Chen, I can and I am closing your store today. I could write you a ticket for every violation on these forms, but I'm giving you a chance to straighten out this mess. Do you understand what I'm saying?"

Ms. Chen replied, "But it no fair. I good person. We sell good food."

I said, "That may be true, but not today. I'm going to finish inspecting the rest of the food court shops and you can start cleaning up this mess. You also need to find cooks who know what they are doing if you want to serve food here."

Ms. Chen was resigned, "I do what you say, but I no like it."

I could hear Ms. Chen fly into another rage as I closed Ping Pow's door behind me and headed down the corridor to my next inspection. News of Ping Pow's misfortune preceded me to every other shop and they were all in exceptionally good form when I arrived. I have never inspected cleaner eateries or been treated with more respect by managers.

Ping Pow did not reopen that day, but they were back in action the next morning with a new cooking crew and a cleaner environment. Barring a complaint, I would not have to deal with Ms. Chen again for several months. I'm sure that made her happy.

I could not have made a hastier departure if the hounds of
hell had been chomping at my heels.

CHAPTER 19
ASHES TO ASHES

During my health inspector days the State of Texas required
that crematoriums be located in a cemetery. This was a fairly ancient
edict, which had great merit when most graveyards were located far
out in the boondocks or at the very least on the edge of town.

As small towns begin to grow and look for space they tend
to annex adjacent properties at an alarming rate. In the mad rush to
acquire more taxable terrain less than ideal acreage often gets sucked
into the fold purely in the interest of expanding the city limits. The
hallowed burial grounds that were once secluded wind up smack in
the middle of housing subdivisions.

Normally the dearly departed make ideal neighbors, if you
are not prone to getting the heebie-jeebies when in close proximity
to the dead. The deceased do not throw wild parties, keep obnoxious
pets, steal your paper, peep in your windows or borrow your stuff.

A well cared for place of final rest may actually increase
the desirability of surrounding lots and elevate property values by
lending a peaceful air to the neighborhood. It could be looked upon

as a meticulously landscaped park, without the noise and confusion created by the living at play, or a lush green golf course without the cursing.

I firmly believe that where people choose to live is solely their business, but I maintain very little compassion for those that move into an area with no regard for how the immediate surroundings will affect them. If you knowingly move into a flood plain and the water inundates your home, the rest of us should not have to bail you out. If you choose a home by an airport, expect those big shiny things that come and go from the sky at all hours to make a lot of racket. Should you select an abode near a cemetery, it may have a working crematory.

Being acutely sensitive to the feelings of ever encroaching homeowners, the operators of the Bliss Crematory attempted to carry out all their work under the cover of darkness. But people would up and die at the most inopportune times and when a number of people departed this earth coincidentally the night shift would be overwhelmed. To meet the demands and time constraints of surviving kinfolk the crematory would have to operate during daylight hours and that would stir up the locals.

Most complaints and inquiries were the direct result of visible smoke emanating from the crematory's chimney. This had a disquieting effect on its witnesses and resulted in some of the most memorable questions I've ever had to field like: "If it gets in my house will I be haunted by spirits?" "Will that smoke take the paint off my car?" "Do you think the smoke is the reason my cat is acting strangely?" "Won't it pollute the lake?" "Should we evacuate until it's over?" "Will it make me sick?" And a real stumper asked by a little girl, "Is that how those people get to heaven?"

The bulk of those concerns were handled on the phone using

simple logic and pointing out that the folks at the crematory had been doing their thing for forty years and no evil spirits or plague had ever been unleashed upon the land. However, when a frail voice called me to report that they were piling ashes outside the crematorium and she felt, "That is just not right with God!" I knew I was headed for a graveyard inspection.

I drove down a quarter mile of single-lane blacktop road into the heart of the cemetery where the crematory sat nestled in a small grove of old pine trees. Long cobalt blue shadows obscured the building from the early morning winter sun. The crematory's smokestack was emitting a gray streak straight into the heavens in the stillness of the new day. The place looked abandoned. I eased around the south side of the building and discovered a four-foot tall pile of ashes against the wall with coffin lids piled at each end. It gave me a chill.

I approached the side doors looking for clues. There were no windows in the small building and its double doors had no locks or knobs. A massive logging chain had been run through the holes where the missing hardware should have been and it was secured with a hefty padlock. The outside gas meter hissed wildly and I could hear the roar of the furnace inside. I stood frozen in front of those doors and watched as they slowly heaved in and out straining against the chains. The doors expanded and contracted in a measured rhythm as if the building were breathing. I could not have made a hastier departure if the hounds of hell had been chomping at my heels.

I chuckled at myself when the goose bumps subsided as I sped away from the crematory. I drove to the funeral parlor on the interstate to talk to the crematory's owners. Surely there was a logical reason for the giant piles of ashes I'd seen.

The receptionist led me to a waiting room and the somber owner of the funeral parlor floated in minutes after she left wearing the blackest suit I'd ever seen. He was tall and gaunt with a pallid complexion. His hands slowly formed geometric shapes as he spoke. He asked, "May I be of service?" while bringing his fingers to a pyramid at his chest.

I did not feel compelled to relate all of my morning's exploits, but I definitely wanted some answers regarding the ash pile. What I would receive was a lesson in cremation. I explained what I'd discovered at one end of his crematory and he listened intently before launching into a measured response using a low monotone with a well-worn cadence.

Outlining rectangular shapes in the air he said, "Our departed loved ones are placed in special caskets designed to be consumed by the extraordinarily hot fires of the crematory along with the bodies they contain. The decorative lids of the caskets, used for aesthetic value during the services, are removed prior to cremation. The ashes you discovered were the residue from the incinerated coffins."

I started to speak, but he froze me with an icy stare and drew squares in front of my face as he continued, "The decorative lids are made exactly like those found on a regular casket and therefore would not burn efficiently. It would be ghastly to reuse them so they are stored with the ashes until enough accumulate to warrant a trip to a disposal site."

As if on cue the laconic receptionist wafted into the room carrying a small box and handed it to the mortician. He droned on, "We remove any valuables or clothing requested by the family from the deceased prior to cremation. A surprisingly small amount of ash and several tiny bones are usually all that remain to be collected and placed in a container like this one."

He then handed me the plastic box with simulated wood grain, which was the budget version of the clichéd vase on the mantel. I shook the box and could hear the muffled rattle of what I presumed to be the remnants of a recently departed customer.

The mortician smiled which resulted in a thin line across his face and no other signs of expression. He continued, "The ashes produced by the deceased and those of the burned coffin are quite different in color and texture. It is not difficult to discern between the two and collect only the individual's remains for return to the family. Feel free to inspect the contents of the box and you will quickly see the difference in what you hold in your hand and what you saw in the cemetery."

I declined his invitation to peek into the box and handed it back to him. He noted my involuntary shudder with indifference. I said, "Would it be too much of a problem for you to store the coffin ashes and lids out of sight so people won't see them and freak out?"

The mortician's eyes gazed into the void for several seconds before he focused them on me and answered, "I believe we can make arrangements that will be deemed suitable for everyone." He extended his arm toward me and slowly swung it toward the exit.

I needed no more cues to leave the funeral parlor and showed great restraint by not bolting for the door. I thanked the mortician for his help as I walked away. The receptionist had abandoned her post and I let myself out. Even on a cold day the sun felt good and I was happy to be alive.

After seven years of being the Mom for an entire city, I was getting tired of telling people to clean up their acts.

CHAPTER 20
STATUS QUO
◆◆◆

Health and Code Enforcement had grown to four full-time health inspectors and three code enforcement officers by my seventh year on the job. As Rex's assistant, Jocko was spending most of his time herding the troops at the Critter Care Center and Rex had become Barney Belcher's sidekick.

The health inspectors had done their best to unload everything that wasn't food service related onto the code enforcement officers. Unless it was an emergency, involved the delicate finessing of a city council member or required placating a politically connected complainer, I was rarely troubled by grass and weeds, unsightly material, inoperative vehicles, swimming pools, fences or signs. With the explosion of new restaurants, retail food sellers, schools, day cares and specialty shops there was still more than enough to make us run to keep up, but the daily grind was becoming routine.

The stench of fetid grease hit me before I could even turn off the air conditioner and climb out of my compact truck. Inspectors were driving their own vehicles now and the city was paying them a monthly stipend. I was parked at the delivery entrance behind one of those huge "all you can eat" Mexican food restaurants. Years of dragging lard soaked trash bags of table scraps and throwing greasy mop water out the back door had left the concrete black where the fat had soaked into it and then been baked day after day by a merciless sun.

It was already unbearably hot at 9:00 AM and just another steamy day in a long string that began in August. For weeks the nighttime temperatures had failed to dip below ninety degrees and triple-digit days left me longing for any kind of breeze, but the winds had taken up residence in cooler climes and there would be no relief from the unrelenting heat until fall arrived.

Earlier this morning I had mistakenly positioned myself in the Chief's line of sight while filing reports. He was looking right at me when a complaint call came through to his desk. This should not have been my problem, but Rex had an extremely simple and efficient method of delegating, so here I was.

I rang the service bell several times before a Latino face peered through the tiny window in the back door and yelled, "Que?" I held up my I.D. and badge. He shouted over his shoulder and took plenty of time before opening the door. I could hear the flurry of activity that started behind him. When my doorman unbarred the entry he retreated into the kitchen before I even stepped across the slippery threshold. Only minutes had passed, but I was sure that everyone in the restaurant knew I was there.

Salsa music blared from a beat-up and food-splattered boom box on a stainless steel prep table at the far end of the well-lit kitchen. A small army of dishwashers, prep cooks, chefs and wait staff scurried around tables piled high with raw vegetables and meat. The floors and walls were covered with red quarry tiles, which already had a greasy film even though they had been pressure washed after closing last night. The culprits causing the room's slick glaze were seven commercial deep fryers, which had been fired up before dawn and were now producing corn chips by the garbage can loads.

The kitchen was stifling. It was too hot and too crowded to move easily and in minutes I felt dirty. A harried looking manager materialized from the chaos. He was full of apologies for not having greeted me sooner. I knew his daily countdown had begun and he had a million details to tend to before his doors opened at 11:00 AM and a steady stream of hungry working class patrons poured into his establishment expecting prompt service and heaps of hot food for four dollars and ninety-nine cents. I dismissed him with a wave, but assured him that we would talk when I had completed my complaint investigation.

I opened my briefcase on a small shelf by the time clock. The place was a beehive of activity. Workers who would ordinarily be outside taking smoking breaks at this time were performing extra chores to make everything look good for my benefit. I knew how much that endeared them to me.

I located the slip of paper the Chief had handed me on my way out of the office and tried to decipher his notoriously illegible handwriting. How I missed Pam Hayes' neat handwriting, but she had retired shortly after we left the old jail.

The complainant was a lady from one of the many small towns north of Bliss. She had stopped with her family on the way to the Dallas Boat Show to eat at our Taco Terrifico. She had been up all night with her daughter who had suffered through the systematic evacuation of her upper and lower units. Because this was the last place they had eaten before enduring their traumatic night she was positive that Taco Terrifico was the source of her daughter's malady.

Unfortunately she had waited two days to notify the Bliss Health Department. In a joint like this, with immense volume and a rapid turnover rate of the daily-prepared products, there would be nothing remotely connected to the batch of food her daughter had consumed. It was a cold trail but a familiar path. I washed my hands and went to work.

The essential tools of my trade are few, but astonishingly revealing. With just a pocket thermometer, mini-flashlight, chemical test strips, pen and clipboard I could poke, prod and peer my way into the very essence of how any restaurant was operated. A practiced eye and a curious nature would open-up any hidden secrets that could have lead to the unsuspecting diner's distress.

One hour later I was on my way back to the office with a full page of only minor violations. I had worked with the manager at Taco Terrifco many times in the past and he knew what he was doing. There would always be plenty of extra cleaning to be performed in his restaurant, but his food handling practices were sound and up to code requirements.

I would have to call my complainant with the sad news that Taco Terrifico wasn't a death trap. She would not want to hear that her little darling may have succumbed to a simple stomach bacterium, fell prey to something she'd eaten earlier in the day, reacted to the amount of spices she'd consumed at the restaurant or even got sick from junk she ate at the Boat Show. Reluctantly I dialed vomit Mom's number and she answered after the first ring.

I fumbled to find her name on the complaint form and asked, "Ms. Warfield?"

Ms. Warfield answered, "Yes, who is this?"

I went into the routine spiel, "Ms. Warfield my name is Ross Ryan and I'm a health inspector with the City of Bliss. I went out to investigate your complaint on Taco Terrifico this morning. I'm…"

She cut me off in mid-sentence with, "I hope you shut that nasty place for good! Their food is awful and it nearly killed my daughter!"

I eased back into my explanation, "Ms. Warfield, I didn't uncover any major violations this morning. There were quite a few minor infractions, but nothing dire enough to shut them down. I made…"

Ms. Warfield stepped in again, "You have got to be kidding me! Didn't they tell you how sick my daughter was? How could you let that place go on serving poison to innocent children?"

I took a deep breath and answered, "Ms. Warfield, I assure you that I made a very thorough inspection of that facility. I didn't find any temperature violations, bad food or problems that could be considered flagrant enough to close them down."

Ms. Warfield blew up on me, "You are one of those countless city employees who don't know what you're doing and don't care about taxpayers like me. You are a fundamental part of what's wrong with this country today. I know that dreadful taco place poisoned my daughter and you have the nerve to call me and say you don't plan to do a darn thing about it?"

I said, "Ms. Warfield, did any of your other family members who ate at Taco Terrifico that night come down with the same symptoms as your daughter or complain about not feeling well?"

There was silence on Ms. Warfield's end of the line as she built up steam for a final barrage, "No, they did not, because they are not fragile little girls! You can bet your butt that your city manager is going to get a letter from me, Mister Ryan!"

I would have been willing to bet that the force of the impact by her receiver damaged the phone when she slammed it down to hang up on me. I was also pretty sure that the city manager would hear about my colossal ineptitude. The rewards of public service are truly innumerable.

After seven years of being the Mom for an entire city, I was getting tired of telling people to clean up their acts. The challenge of dealing one-on-one with the general public, business people and fellow professionals had not abated, but the context had become numbing.

Career advancement within the Health Department was not an option. Rex was so far in debt with ex-wives, child support, medical bills and the constant need for new cars that he would be forced to continue working until they hauled him away on a stretcher. Jocko was firmly entrenched as Rex's assistant leaving me doomed to accept a two- or three- percent pay increase each year for mostly mucking through kitchens.

The Personnel Department Head position became vacant and Barney Belcher briefly envisioned incorporating another department into his Community Development dynasty. I had four years of Personnel Department experience on my resume from Snow Mountain Ranch during my ski-bum days, and Barney thought I should take a run at acquiring the job.

Dick Darling had a young cocksure assistant city manager that was doing the interviewing for the personnel spot. I was granted an interview out of courtesy to Barney. I had caused Dick's assistant to feel embarrassed in front of some female employees at an after hours bar party, when he tampered with the balls during my pool game and he assured me that I would never rise above my current job level. I did not clear the first cut for the personnel spot, and Dick's assistant went on to another city where he was rumored to have committed a breach of ethics and was instructed to leave.

The Fire Marshal, Red Ferrel, had the only remaining assistant's position in the city and it had never been filled since Dick created it. My knowledge of fire prevention was as lacking as my experience at being a health inspector when I first started, but I was a seasoned veteran in the game of city politics and could be trusted. Red had no other real prospects and was afraid the council would cut the position if he did not fill it soon.

Dick's new assistant, Clyde Regal, turned out to be a genuinely good character and was actually known to venture up from the first floor to the circus on the second level from time to time. Clyde had no problem with Red hiring me, Rex gave my promotion to management his blessing, and I became the Assistant Fire Marshal for the City of Bliss.

Successfully firing a city employee is rarer than an Immaculate Conception.

CHAPTER 21

FIRE PREVENTION

Barney Belcher was the Bliss Fire Marshal when he hired Red Ferrel. Red immediately became Barney's fair-haired boy and his designated replacement when Barney was crowned the Community Development Grand Puba. Barney planned for Red to graduate from Fire Marshal to Puba one day and began grooming Red for the position by dumping the majority of his workload squarely in Red's lap.

Red desperately needed an assistant as the crush of responsibility from performing his and Barney's job duties slowly overwhelmed him. Barney was rapidly approaching R.O.J. status, which was city government speak for "retired on the job."

Sharon Moran and Della Stern were Red's lead Fire Inspectors. They were two no-nonsense ladies, half-again as old as Red and adored working for him. Sharon and Della had been city employees for so many years that they had dirt on everyone and were smart enough to know better than to use it.

A young punk named Ricky Spoons, replaced Red's third

fire inspector just prior to my accepting the Assistant Fire Marshal position. Spoons had done a short hitch in the army and stayed only long enough to become a proficient slacker. Red had hired Spoons as the result of political pressure from the City Attorney, who was best buds with Spoons' dad.

Sharon and Della took their jobs very seriously, as well they should have. Keeping people from burning up themselves and their possessions is weighty work. They made no effort to hide their contempt for Spoons flippant disregard for the job and his constant efforts to avoid doing any actual labor. Della became especially obsessed with exposing Spoons' incompetence to the point of it affecting her own performance. I inherited dissension among the ranks from day one.

Since Spoons and I were new to the world of Fire Prevention we would have to attend classes authorized by the State of Texas to earn our credentials. For one week of every month we drove to nearby Farlington to endure the minutia of fire inspecting tedium.

Men with potbellies and handlebar mustaches who seemed to place more weight on discussing historical conflagrations and firehouse anecdotes than actual inspecting practices and related codes taught my fire prevention courses. The room was full of fire fighters who were crossing over to the prevention side because they needed to work regular hours or they had been relegated the role to satisfy vague insurance requirements tied to reducing their municipalities' key rates. Fire Prevention was looked upon as a bastard child of most Fire Departments and a drain on finances that could be allocated for new trucks and gear. I learned far more from Sharon and Della while performing my actual fire prevention duties than I ever got from six weeks of state mandated training.

What I did learn from the fire fighters that gathered weekly in Farlington was how to escalate lunchtime to a memorable event. Farlington was a tourist trap geared solely toward parting people from their entertainment dollars. Farlington had giant amusement parks, lavish golf courses, countless restaurants, lots of hotels and the finest strip clubs in north Texas.

Due to the thinness of our course curriculum, the bubbas who presided over our training allocated two hours for us to eat lunch every day. We would leave class at 11:00 AM and arrive at Luscious Ladies as they were opening the doors for business. Luscious Ladies put out a free buffet every day from 11:00 AM to 1:00 PM and the food was always hot, filling and not half-bad. Luscious Ladies required a two-drink minimum to partake in the buffet, but two glasses of iced tea, that cost four dollars each, satisfied their demands and still made lunch a bargain.

The girls that worked the early shift at Luscious Ladies were all college coeds financing their educations by dropping their drawers and raking in dollars from thankful old codgers who felt blessed to be in their naked presence. The fire prevention troops were made to feel extra welcome during our one week a month visits. The girls began their workdays by sitting down at our tables and eating off the buffet with us. They made interesting mealtime conversationists as we discussed their studies and future employment plans. When they finished their meals they stood up, took their clothes off and began dancing. The result was a fine dining experience indeed, which gave special meaning to the old saw, "a meal and more." Our eagerness to attend fire prevention training each week confused Red and the gals back in Bliss, but I had sworn Spoons to secrecy and not telling was the one thing he ever did that pleased me while on the job.

I plunged into the piles of building codes, fire codes and city ordinances that pertained to the Fire Prevention Division's activities. Red shed his plan review chores for new construction of buildings and left me to flounder with the requirements for fire sprinklers, vent hood extinguishing systems, stand pipes, exits, alarms, signs and fire lanes. Red said I should dig through the codes and make my own decisions on fire related requirements, which meant he had plenty to do without holding my hand and expected me to come up to speed quickly.

In college I minored in Industrial Arts, which gave me a leg up in reviewing and understanding building plan submittals. I was still a little less than fully prepared for the intricacies involved with the construction of The Big Orange Hardware Store. The building's fire sprinkler system was a maze of thousands of feet of black pipe with requirements for special sprinkler heads and hose systems to cover the expanse of the warehouse floor and beefed up sections to protect the lumber and flammable liquids they sold in bulk. On paper it looked like an elaborate Rube Goldberg invention and even though I approved the plan within the allotted time, I could make no real sense of the system until it was completed and I went to the store for testing and a final okay. Fortunately, Big Orange was a nationwide chain and this was not their first large project.

While I was attempting to educate myself in all things Fire Prevention related, the Spoons' situation continued to fester. Since I would have to perform the annual evaluations for my fire inspectors, I decided I should follow up on some of their recent efforts and see how thorough they had been and how well their customers had received them. It did not take long at all to discover that Spoons was doing an excellent job of filling out forms and filing completed inspection reports with only one small catch, he was not actually performing the work. Building owners, who signed his forms, did not complain because he never asked them to correct any problems or spend any money.

Successfully firing a city employee is rarer than an Immaculate Conception. Della had painstakingly compiled a long list of Spoons' sins, but nobody had ever formally confronted him, disciplined him, filed a formal reprimand with personnel or placed him on a performance improvement plan. His permanent record appeared squeaky clean.

I laboriously wrote out every omitted inspection and falsely filed report that I could document as my own personal discovery while overseeing Spoons' work. When it was all compiled into an ominously official looking document, I took it to the head of personnel for approval. She liked what she saw but said that there had not been enough effort in the past to correct Spoons' actions and the most I could do was reprimand him and put him on a plan for improvement.

I decided to gamble on Spoons' military background to work in my favor. Just before five on a Thursday I called Spoons into my office, closed the door and confronted him with my big book of bad news regarding his lack of job performance. In the army a bad record can dog a man the rest of his life and enlisted men learned early to avoid permanent blemishes. I let Spoons thumb through my pages of accusations and started in with, "I'm sure you are aware that your performance has not been deemed satisfactory for a long time."

Spoons looked up at me briefly, mouthed a quiet, "Has it?" and went back to scanning my accusations.

I continued, "As a fire inspector you are charged with the public's trust to perform your duties to the best of your ability to keep people safe from fire related disasters. Failing to check for things like working fire extinguishers, blocked exits, functioning sprinkler systems and proper alarms could cause someone to be killed in an emergency situation."

Perspiration began to form in beads on Spoons' forehead. He sat the thick sheaf of offenses on my desk and looked up at me. I stood behind my desk and launched into my best evangelist's timbre. "What you've been doing is inexcusable. Think about the legal ramifications and your own personal guilt if somebody would have died because of your negligence. These documents have not been filed with personnel yet, but when they are it will be your butt on the line if a catastrophe occurs before we can go back and recheck all your work."

Spoons' eyebrows arched and there was a glimmer of hope in his eyes. He asked, "So these documents aren't in my personnel file yet?"

He took the bait and I knew I had him. I leaned across my desk, resting on both palms and said, "No, but they will be by tomorrow. I have a copy for you to read through and sign saying you received and understand them. Then they go to personnel."

Spoons squirmed in his seat, cocked his head to one side and asked, "But what if I don't sign them?"

I replied, "Then I make a note of that and file them anyway. The way I see this thing playing out you have three options: You can sign these papers and we start you on a plan closely documenting each step of your improvement, I could fire you or you can turn in your resignation. Now get out of my office and go home. I want you to think long and hard about your future with Bliss."

Spoons somberly walked out of my office as if he carried the weight of the world on his irresponsible shoulders. It was after 5:00 PM and the second floor was deserted. I peered out of my office window and spotted him getting into his car in the parking lot. Even his driving was slow and methodical when he pulled onto Main Street and putted away.

The next morning Spoons was waiting for me in my office when I arrived. He handed me a sloppily typed sheet of paper and exclaimed, "I've decided to resign."

I took the page and picked up the phone. Thankfully the personnel director, Jana Dukes, had come in early and answered. She agreed to personally start processing Spoons' exit papers and I sent him downstairs.

On his way out the door Spoons turned and said, "My Dad has found another job for me where I'll make twice as much money and work a lot less. I think this happened at a good time for me."

Spoons was a preeminent prevaricator and I could not imagine him being employed and actually getting paid to do less work. I gave him a cheerful grin and said, "I think you made a splendid decision and I truly believe this will work out the best for everyone."

When Della Stern got to work and saw that Spoons had cleaned out his desk in their shared cubicle she was beside herself with joy. For Della it was a banner day and worthy of celebration at the highest level. It was good to have her back on track and in good spirits.

The search for Spoons' replacement began immediately. It seemed like every city department had employees that wanted a shot at the Fire Prevention Officer's job. Even people from the first floor at the Civic Center sent in their applications. It was overwhelming.

The fire prevention field is comprised of a tight group and word got out fast that Bliss had an opening. Red wanted no part of interviewing and filling the vacant post. He was still gun-shy after the Spoons debacle. With hundreds of applications to choose from there were surprisingly few that had any real experience and the state required credentials to take the job and start contributing immediately.

The only really qualified candidate was a man who lived in Austin, Texas, named Pete Rippledoodle. Red laughed out loud when I told him I'd called Rippledoodle in for an interview. Red shook his head and said, "If he has survived with that name, he's got to be tough."

North Texas isn't known for massive snowstorms, but paralyzing ice storms wreak legendary havoc in the area at least once a winter. The Texas landscape was a solid sheet of ice from Austin to Bliss the day Rippledoodle was scheduled to appear. I had potential interviewees call in and cancel from as little as ten miles away and I could not blame any of them. Rippledoodle called in, but it was to give me an up-date on his progress every couple of hours and let me know he was still coming. Pete Rippledoodle arrived at my office at 4:45 PM for a 10:00 AM appointment, and I could not have been more impressed by his effort. I offered Rippledoodle the job after chatting with him for just an hour and he was a proud addition to our team that I never regretted.

I finished the last three years of my ten-year Bliss career working with Red, Sharon, Della and Pete in the Fire Prevention Division as the city's first and only Assistant Fire Marshal. I tagged

Pete with the nickname, Paladin, because he was always on the spot in emergencies and Rippledoodle was too darn funny to use in serious discourse. I had only moved several dozen steps down the aisle from my Health Inspector's position, but the change in environment made it well worth the trip.

We heard a ferocious metal on metal clang and wheeled to see the fully pressurized hose flailing wildly through the air creating arcing rainbows in the summer sun and massive gashes in Jessie's Ford.

CHAPTER 22
FIRE INSPECTIONS

Performing fire inspections was no more complicated than conducting health inspections; it just required the knowledge of a whole new set of rules and regulations. The fact that I was a novice was not a major hindrance in testing newly installed fire apparatus unless the contractor was also new at the game. If we were both experimenting, trouble was bound to ensue.

I arrived early for my first fire hydrant flow test. Red had given me a ten-minute introduction, I had read the relevant sections in the National Fire Prevention Association's (NFPA) codes and I was armed with an official fire hydrant wrench. The hydrant to be tested was situated on top of a ten-inch water main and I was sure to discover enough pressure for the required fire sprinkle system to be installed in a new restaurant near the mall.

The contractor arrived in a shiny new Ford pickup that still had the dealer's sticker in the passenger window of its crew cab. Buildings were going up so fast that new hires were needed in every facet of the construction industry and we were both proof of that maxim. Jessie Gonzales parked his new rig near our test hydrant, stepped out and introduced himself to me, "Hi, I'm the guy with Fast Fire Protection."

I shook his hand and replied, "I'm Ross Ryan with the city of Bliss."

Jessie retrieved a flow test gauge and a hydrant wrench from his truck and set them by the test plug. He went back and got a twenty-five foot section of three-inch fire hose that was rolled as if it had just come from a firehouse. I was about to inquire about the hose's purpose when Jessie said, "This here is my first hydrant test in the field. My boss said that this hydrant is new and I should give it a good flush before we put the gauge on it. I figured to use the hose to divert the water away from us while we let it run a spell."

It sounded good to me so I agreed. Jessie removed a side cap and hooked up his curly hose. He rolled it out parallel with the road, and I was surprised to see it reach past his parked truck. Jessie adjusted his wrench to fit the hydrant's valve on top and began gingerly turning to open the hydrant. We'd both been warned not to open the hydrant quickly and risk a sudden slam of water pressure that could damage it and the water line so we concentrated on the task at hand. With our backs to Jessie's truck, what we did not expect was that hose thrashing the bejabbers out of his new rig. We heard a ferocious metal on metal clang and wheeled to see the fully pressurized hose flailing wildly through the air creating arcing rainbows in the summer sun and massive gashes in Jessie's Ford. By the time Jessie could react to this fiasco and shut the hydrant down his truck had sustained a cracked windshield and half a dozen crescent dents in the hood, roof and door. We observed a mutual moment of silence as the now limp hose lay on the pavement draining.

Jessie spoke first, "Man, I sure didn't see that coming."

We surveyed the damage on his battered ride and it looked much worse from close up. The hose had slashed through the metal in some of the deeper dents. With wide eyes Jessie said, "Well, at least that thing didn't kill one of us." We finished the test without further incident and both developed a great respect for the force a fire hydrant's water pressure can create.

My second fire hydrant test occurred in a vacant field where a new housing subdivision would soon blossom. I was in a state of heightened alert for this test and keeping a vigilant eye on all equipment and people around the test area to avoid any property destruction.

I had positioned myself in what I considered the safest of possible spots and gave the go ahead nod to the two gentlemen from Water Works Safety to open the hydrant. They were standing on opposite sides of the fire hydrant passing the wrench to each other as they slowly opened the valve. Water had just begun to gush forth in a thick stream at low pressure when suddenly a blinding rush of searing pain ran up both legs clear to my naughty bits. I screamed in terror like a girlie man and looked down to discover the lower half of my body consumed in fire ants. The Water Works Safety boys looked up from their task to find me stripping out of my shoes, socks and pants while running toward them. I dashed into the hydrant's flow whipping wildly at the tiny tormentors stinging my legs. I stood for several minutes in the flowing water and my soggy boxers after all the ants had been washed away reveling in the soothing coolness.

As the terror and pain subsided the reality of my situation returned to me as if I was waking from an awful nightmare. Both the men from Water Works Safety were doubled over in laughter. I just couldn't care at that point. They were still chuckling when I retrieved my clothes and we finished up the test. I didn't blame them; if my legs hadn't stung so bad I, too, would have been laughing uncontrollably.

I had not completely escaped the grit and grease of kitchens by joining Fire Prevention. Commercial kitchen vent hoods are required to have automatic fire extinguishing systems, and they have to be tested periodically and when first installed. Fires erupting from cooking surfaces are expected to involve flammable liquids so vent hood systems are designed to release chemical agents to extinguish such blazes. They are triggered when a fusible link melts allowing a spring-loaded lever to dump their cylinders.

The manager at Wee Willy Day Care let me in the back door and told me that the technician from Fire Guard was in the kitchen. I walked in to find Jack Bone standing on a ten-burner stove handing the metal filters from a vent hood to his new assistant, Gordo. Jack's boots and pants were caked from years of grease coating and Gordo was working toward the same look. Jack jumped down from the stove and thrust out a permanently blackened hand, which I hesitantly shook.

Jack said, "You must be Ryan. Sharon and Della done told me all about you."

I replied, "Oh, really?"

Jack went on, "Yeah, I been working with those two for longer than I can remember. I'm Jack and this here's Gordo. Gordo is just gettin' started, but I think he'll make a good technician."

Gordo gave me a nod and went on about his work. Jack pointed at the system's big red cylinders and informed me that, "Gordo's already replaced them two cylinders. They was out of date." He picked up an older looking cylinder from the floor by the stove and showed me an expired date stamped into its bottom. It was the first time I'd looked at one of these systems for how it was supposed to work instead of writing down how badly it needed to be cleaned. I was thankful that Jack knew what he was doing.

Jack sat the bottle down and pointed at a piece of metal connecting a taught wire. He explained, "That there is where a fusible link goes. It melts if there's a fire." He removed an example from his pocket for me to examine and went on, "I got a test link in there for now. What we'll do is cut that so you can see the trigger wire spring and we got it connected to an air tank to blow the caps off the nozzles so you can see the pipes are clear and the thing is in proper working order."

He pulled a pair of wire cutters from his tool belt and gave me a little shove with the back of his hand. As he was reaching up to cut the test link he said, "You should stand back so as not to get hit with any wire or pieces of test link that might fly off when she springs."

There was a slight click when Jack snipped the test link, then a loud bang, followed by a mighty whoosh and the whole kitchen turned white. I began to gag. I could not see a thing, but I heard Jack yell, "Gordo, you idiot!" Gordo had hooked up the new tanks instead of the test cylinder, and we'd coated the entire kitchen with fifty pounds of fine, white dust.

Jack was only standing a few feet away, but it was several minutes before the air cleared enough for me to see him. His eyes and mouth formed dark holes in his powdered white face when he said, "Well, that's how they work."

White powder puffed in front of my face when I laughed and said, "That was one heck of a demonstration."

Jack shook his head and replied, "I can't say that's the first one of these things I've accidentally dumped, but you're the first inspector I've dusted. I'm awful sorry about that. You're gonna want to go home and shower that stuff off pretty quick; it could cause you some irritation. We'll get this place cleaned up and call when we get ready to try again."

Jack was still yelling at Gordo when I left the kitchen. There were several children who saw me leave that derived great joy from my powder-coated look. I could hear one child yell, "Was that a ghost?" as the rear door closed behind me. Traces of powder turned up in my briefcase and truck for months after my unexpected dusting, and it always made me laugh.

Fire alarm systems in hospitals, schools or industrial facilities can be extremely complex so I decided to cut my teeth at a day care facility. Bliss was building kiddy-keeping establishments by the dozen and they all were required to install fire alarm systems.

News of my exploits at Wee Willy Day Care had preceded me when I arrived at Tiny Tots and was greeted by the manager. She said, "I hope you're not here to do the kitchen."

I said, "No. I'm here to test the fire alarm system."

She snickered and said, "That's a relief, it's almost time to make lunch."

The alarm technician walked in behind me and introduced himself, "Hi, I'm Albert. I hope I'm not late."

I said, "I just arrived myself."

Albert said, "Good. Let's get after it." He looked at the manager and asked, "Is this alarm hooked up to go off site and notify the fire department?"

The manager said, "Yes, why?"

Albert instructed her, "I want you to call the fire department and tell them we are testing your alarm so they won't send any emergency vehicles."

The manager went into her office to call and Albert and I opened up the fire alarm's control panel and got to work. Albert pointed at a battery and explained, "That's the back-up in case the power goes out." He pulled a tester from his bag and the battery showed good. Then he said, "Let's start with the farthest detector and work our way back to the box. You stay here and I'll go set off the detector. When the indicator comes on write down that it passed and reset the alarm for the next test."

I said, "Got it." and Albert walked down the hall toward the day room.

In just a few minutes the alarm went off and the proper indicator lit up. I marked it off the list, reset the alarm and waited for the next test. Before the second detector could be activated I heard sirens in the distance. Albert came trotting down the hall and said, "Oh, no. Don't tell me they're coming here."

We both walked out the front door and stood in the parking lot. In moments two engines and an ambulance raced into the lot and screeched to a halt. Out jumped several firemen and they slowed as Albert and I held our arms up to stop them.

The Captain was shaking his head as he walked toward me. He asked, "Are you testing that alarm?"

I wanted to be anywhere else, but stood there and said, "Yes.

The manager was supposed to call, but…"

The Captain continued to shake his head and launched into quite a detailed dressing down on my behalf. It was all about my imperiling his men and other people's lives while they raced around town thinking children were about to burn to death. He was still going at it when one of the men called from his engine and said, "Captain, we got another call to make."

As they were pulling away Albert said, "That's why I asked if the alarm went off site. They don't take kindly to false alarms."

The manager at the day care had gotten sidetracked by a mother who called to ask about her child and never notified the fire department. Albert and I both learned to make the call ourselves in the future. As a matter of fact, Bliss Fire Prevention put a new rule in place requiring inspectors to call dispatch on their radios before testing any equipment that had an alarm. This dramatically reduced the elevation of blood pressure in angry fire captains during livid oratories.

My toe had begun to throb again, my back and arms ached
and I stunk of lake slime.

CHAPTER 23

FLASH FISHING

Red Ferrel acquired a hand-me-down aluminum fishing boat that had belonged to Gene Autrey's dad. It was a fourteen-footer from Spears with leaky rivets and a finicky outboard that was older than Red. The boat had been forgotten at its mooring on a pond that belonged to Gene's father. Years of rain and neglect had caused the little craft to disappear in the mud only to resurface during a prolonged drought. Gene retrieved the boat and gave it to Red because it was too sorry to sell.

Red cleaned up the resurrected vessel and found a weathered trailer to fit its stumpy dimensions. The little boat's dubious past should have been a harbinger of things to come, but a free boat is hard to turn down even if it is an ugly duckling. Red named the boat "Flash."

With Lake Bliss on our doorstep the temptation to go fishing in its murky waters was irresistible. Red and I made several excursions in Flash that were noteworthy only for being giant fiascos producing no fish. Ample amounts of beer were consumed on hot summer days plying Lake Bliss's waters in search of big bass, but the end results were always a bust.

I was at the Little Dallas Marina on Lake Bliss sweating profusely in the aft bilge of my sailboat attempting to tighten lower gudgeon bolts that had been knocked loose when my rudder discovered a tree stump during a midnight cruise. The sound of small waves lapping the outside of my stern was drowned out by the coughing approach of a small outboard. I felt a thump against the stern and the hacking motor wheezed to a stop.

From outside Red yelled, "Hey, Ryan, are you in there?"

I yelled back through the sailboat's thick fiberglass, "Yeah, I'm down in the bottom of this bucket trying to keep her rudder from falling off."

I could hear Red laugh and he yelled back, "Let's go fishing. It's too hot to work on that thing and there's no wind anyway."

I climbed out of my boat's dark innards and into the sunlight. It was ninety-five degrees, but it felt much cooler out in the open air. There Red sat in Flash holding onto my stern ladder. I attempted to bow out of the fishing trip, "I don't have any fishing equipment on board."

Red pointed at rods and reels laying in several inches of water on Flash's bottom and replied, "I've got all the gear we need. Besides I've got a cooler full of cold beer and it doesn't feel nearly as hot out on the open lake."

He had me there and I said, "Let me button up my boat and I'll go." I put the drop boards in the companionway, slid the hatch closed and padlocked the entry to the sailboat. I climbed down onto the dock into Flash's bow seat. It took several pulls, but Red got the testy outboard started and we putted from the back of the marina toward open water.

We were headed down the main marina fairway when I saw an eighteen-foot, yellow ski boat tied to one of the slips by the gas dock. It was far from unusual for a visiting boat to be moored there, but women surrounded this boat. There were two gals lounging on the dock at the boat's bow, drinking iced beverages in plastic cups and a tall young lady hovering over the boat's inboard engine next to its cover, which was resting on the seats behind her. As we inched closer a big, burly lady stood up from near the engine with grease on her arms and a bandana around her closely cropped hair.

I turned back to look at Red and said, "Do you figure they're lesbians?" Now sound travels amazingly well over water, and I had inadvertently raised my voice to be heard over the sputtering outboard. Every female head on the dock and in that boat suddenly turned our way.

Red looked terrifically annoyed and said, "Now you've done it, Ryan."

I was embarrassed and hissed back, "Just speed up a little and let's get past them."

Red shook his head and said, "I can't. We have to stop for gas."

Red steered Flash toward the gas pumps at the end of the dock and the tall girl that had been standing in the yellow boat climbed out onto the pier and headed our way. Red killed the engine, leaned forward and whispered to me as we drifted toward the pilings, "She's going to tear you a new one and I'm not getting involved. You brought this on yourself."

The tall girl was towering above me as I tied Flash's bow line to the piling. She leaned down and asked, "Do you guys have any tools? Our boat's broken and Maggie doesn't have the right tool to fix it."

I was relieved that she did not clobber me. I wanted to be helpful, "What kind of tool does she need?"

The tall girl said, "I'm not sure. Would you come over and talk to Maggie?" It sounded like a trap, but there was no way out and guilt was gnawing at me.

Red answered for me, "Sure he will. I'll get gas while you go see what the ladies need, Ross." I clamored up onto the pier and followed the tall girl around the marina store to where the others waited by their boat.

The gals in the lounges were griping at Maggie about having to spend their evening lying on the dock when we arrived. Maggie was on her knees in the floor of the boat with her head near the engine sucking on a clear plastic tube attempting to prime a small electric pump that was laboring to remove an oil and water mixture from the bilge. She stood up, tossed the tube over the side and spat a mouthful of chocolate crud into the lake. Maggie had well toned arms covered with tattoos that would make a marine wince, and she wiped the slime from her mouth with the tail of her sleeveless shirt before asking me, "You got a three-eighths end wrench?"

My eyes were wide, but I tried to sound nonchalant when I replied, "Yes. It's on my sailboat in the back of the marina."

Maggie never unlocked the stare she had on me and explained, "One of these fools put water in the oil filler on this engine. I managed to get the drain plug out with some pliers, but I'm going to need a three-eighths end wrench to drain the heat exchanger. You going to help me with that, or what?"

I knew I was no match for Maggie and wanted to atone for my comment, so I said, "Sure thing. We'll run back and get it for you."

Maggie maintained her gaze and said, "That would be

fine, sport. We'll leave it on the end piling down there when we're done."

Red and I putted back to my boat, got the wrench and delivered it to Maggie before heading out to fish. We had just started to work some submerged brush when Red said, "You know you got off easy even if you never see that wrench again."

I chuckled and replied, "Man, I'd of given her my whole tool box if she wanted it."

We fished for several hours until the sun sank low on the horizon. Red didn't want to pull Flash after dark so he ran me back to the marina before heading home. We didn't catch a fish or even get a bite, but my wrench was sitting on the piling when we returned so our luck hadn't been all bad.

Several weeks passed before Red conned me into another fishing trip. He'd eaten lunch at Ye Olde Meat Shoppe and the local boys were all bragging about the fish they were catching in the creek that flowed into the west end of Bliss Lake. Red said, "There is a little park on that end of the lake with an excellent boat ramp. We could be in the water by 6:00 PM and the guys who always catch fish on this lake swear we'll have a boat full by dark."

I had never caught a fish in Flash, but it was a hot August day and I didn't have anything else to do with my evening but hide from the heat in the air conditioning at home. I agreed to go.

We arrived at the park and had to pay the guard a fee to get past the entry gate. We drove down a gentle grade and rounded the corner where a double boat ramp angled into the water. There was a big turning area and the parking spaces were double long for vehicles pulling trailers. Two ski boats full of teenagers and twenty-somethings were milling around in the water at the end of the ramp waiting for their drivers to park and return. A large deck boat with too much family was on one side of the ramp, and we pulled into the other side where a fancy bass boat had just pulled out.

Red backed the battered trailer down the ramp and I followed on foot holding a bow line. He hit the brakes hard when the trailer submerged and Flash shot off into the water as planned. Red pulled away leaving me standing on the ramp and Flash floating at the end of my line. It was as smooth an unloading as we had ever accomplished and the whole crowd took note of our efforts.

Another expensive bass rig circled into place for unloading and I tugged Flash toward shore. The little aluminum wonder floated to one side of the boat ramp and I stepped off the pavement into the rocks to catch her. In an instant I slipped and fell out of sight in two-feet of water. I tried to regain my footing on the moss-covered rocks as quickly as possible and lurched to my feet with a broad brown brush stroke of slime down my back. I felt sure the big toe on my right foot had been sheared off, but I looked back up the hill to see if Red had witnessed my fall instead of checking on my wound. He was walking toward me and had seen the whole flop.

Red was doing his best not to bust a gut when he arrived at the ramp and asked me through clenched teeth, "Are you OK?"

I was not OK, but all eyes were now on me and I was mortified. I hissed back at Red, "Just get in the boat and let's get out of here."

Red climbed in the back and I shoved us off the rocks and slithered over the bow. My big toe was still there, but it was bleeding from a nasty gash across the bottom where it connected to my foot. I must have slashed it on some glass.

Flash drifted into the path of all the boats trying to load and unload on the ramp. Red began to yank earnestly at the engine's start rope but it was making no effort to fire. We were shoved away by several boats' occupants attempting to keep the drifting aluminum menace from scratching their shiny hulls. Red had removed the outboard's engine cover and we were clinging to some stumps about twenty yards from shore when all the other boats cleared the area. A little cursing, coaxing and a lot more pulling later we were on our way. Our smooth move entry had been dashed, but there were fish to be caught.

We headed out of the cove where the ramp was situated and around the park toward the creek's entrance. Red hit a small stump on the way, but the engine didn't die and we sped onward as if nothing had happened.

We had cruised a mile or so up the creek's main channel before Red killed the outboard and we drifted into some thick treetops. I changed boat ends with Red and he dropped the electric trolling motor over the bow. We worked with all colors of plastic worms, bobbed jigs and threw casting baits until our arms ached as we floated from submerged structure to submerged structure back down the creek and never got a bite. We were exhausted and out of beer by sunset.

Red pulled up the trolling motor and we changed boat ends again. Surprisingly the outboard fired up after half a dozen pulls. Red ran Flash as fast as she would go back down the channel and around the little park's point. He eased back on the boat's throttle just before we entered the cove where the ramp lay and said, "Why don't we give it one more try along that far bank?"

My toe had stopped bleeding and I'd dulled the pain with beer so I agreed. Red steered Flash across the mouth of the cove and into some stumps on the far bank. He hit the kill switch on the engine, which hiccupped and convulsed for several minutes before dying in a spasm.

The wind began to blow us away from the cove, but we were drifting parallel with the bank, which was perfect for casting. I actually hooked a fish on my tenth cast. This was a big fish that doubled my pole over and moved the boat in its direction. We were both stunned by this first bite of the day and I held on for all I was worth, but the fish was gaining line and showing no signs of coming my way. It seemed like a long time, but I'm sure it was only minutes before my line broke and I nearly lurched out of the boat on the opposite side. We both had a fine laugh at my folly and agreed that even a short fish fight in Flash might have been our best showing to date.

It was getting dark and Red started pulling on the outboard's starter cord. Red pulled awhile, then I pulled awhile and then Red took another long turn before we gave into the fact that the engine was not going to run, period. We had drifted about a quarter of a mile from our cove and the breeze was building in our faces. Red dropped the electric trolling motor into the water and we started edging toward our goal.

I said, "Well, it's slow, but at least we're headed in the right direction. I hope you didn't have any dinner plans."

Red looked overly concerned and shot back, "Dinner plans are the least of our worries. That park will close in thirty minutes and we'll be locked in for the night. I hadn't planned on being out here after 10:00 PM, and it's a good three miles to the nearest phone if we have to take a hike."

I was worried now. We both sat quietly as the little trolling motor labored to pull us into the wind and toward home. The batteries lasted about fifteen minutes and we were only halfway to the ramp when the trolling motor faded away.

Red scrounged around in Flash's belly and came up with two small paddles. They were barely long enough to reach the water. He looked at me apologetically and said, "I never really planned to use these things."

We both leaned awkwardly over Flash's sides and began paddling. The little boat was not designed to be propelled by canoe paddles and the going was slow and rough, but we were making headway. We fought it out and glided into the deserted ramp and parking area with minutes to spare. Red ran to get the truck and backed the trailer into the water in record time. I tugged Flash into place, locked her down and we sped for the tollbooth.

The park ranger was locking up the entry gates as we screeched to a halt in front of the exit. He spun around and walked toward us. Red rolled down the window on the driver's side of the truck's cab and the ranger said, "I didn't figure you boys were going to make it out of here tonight. I've been watching you to make sure you were safe, but I try to go home at closing if there isn't an emergency. You guys sure have had a tough time of it."

Red looked at me and we both laughed out loud. He turned to the ranger and said, "Yeah, it hasn't been one of our brighter adventures, but we'd sure like to get home tonight."

The ranger went back to the gate and freed us. My toe had begun to throb again, my back and arms ached and I stunk of lake slime. Red looked as weary as I felt. We made our way down the dark country roads in silence. We were too tired to even listen to the radio.

When we got to Red's house he backed Flash into the

garage. Red lived in one of those subdivisions where something that looked as ugly as Flash was forbidden to remain exposed. I was walking toward my car when Red said, "That was some fishing trip, huh?"

I just shook my head and said, "Yup, and I don't think I ever want to make another one like it."

We were stopped just inside the front door by a massive woman in a flowered muumuu with tattoos of men's anatomy on her arms and no front teeth.

CHAPTER 24
COWPOKES
◆◆◆

The State Highway ran due east out of the Old Town part of Bliss. It paralleled the Bliss Lake dam and there was nothing but huge clumps of mesquite trees and Johnson grass covering the uneven ground between the road and the dam on the north side. The south side was undeveloped farmland that rolled off toward Dallas.

It was a long and lonely stretch of two-lane blacktop before the tiny town of Settlement sprang out of the prairie on the east end of Bliss Lake. Between Settlement and Bliss was no man's land, partner, and inspectors didn't travel that way on business.

Bliss had been careful to draw its city limit line along the north side of the state road to include the entire length of Bliss Lake dam. The Corps of Engineers maintained an office in Bliss, which insured that a continuous flow of federal dollars for maintenance and upkeep passed through the city. The city limit line circled back around a marina at the lake's farthest eastern edge and returned to Bliss proper in the middle of the lake to encompass the city's water intake pipes.

A piece of pie-shaped property was formed between the State Road, the Corps' property and an elevated railroad track at the end of no man's land. A giant metal building had been erected on this property with an asphalt parking lot to match. The steel beam and sheet metal monstrosity was named "Dance Land" and mature patrons went there to cut a rug.

Weekends at Dance Land were filled with ballroom dancing competitions, and the geriatric set that still appreciated a good tango, waltz, or rumba gathered there after the early bird specials. The parking lot would fill with classy old sedans around dusk and empty long before midnight. The place was mostly deserted during the week.

A few miles east of Dance Land the town of Settlement began to swell with young Dallas commuters. The burgeoning flow of yuppies caused massive congestion on the two-lane State Road's unlit blacktop at night, and the aging hoofers began to lose interest in tripping the light fantastic at far away Dance Land. The younger set in Settlement showed no interest in old style cavorting so Dance Land closed, the parking lot became weed infested and another dinosaur slumped in place.

Schemers and dreamers in droves marched into Barney Belcher's Wednesday meetings clutching fantastic plans for revitalizing the old Dance Land property only to face the realization of having to bring the premises up to current codes and standards. Dance Land had no city water or sewer hook-ups and long expensive runs of new pipe would be required to make connections with distant existing mains. The grand size of the place would also require an expensive fire sprinkler system to be installed.

A few plans, which were less grand in scale, did get

approved. A slice was sold off of the east side of the parking lot to build a mini warehouse and the entry and exit drives were repaired to accommodate people with overflow from their stuffed garages. An office for leasing rental trucks was carved out of the east end of the cavernous building, and more traffic began to flow in and out of the abandoned premises.

Mini warehouses and truck leasing offices don't require much strict oversight from the city, but several reports of heightened activity at the old Dance Land grounds began to trickle into Community Development. By the time inspectors were dispatched to check up on the place, a full-blown striptease club was operating in the western half of the big building. They were dancing at Dance Land again, but without their clothes.

The seedy overseers of this bawdry burlesque had done their homework and quietly bought up all the old property rights and business claims from Dance Land's former owners. The city of Bliss had neglected to formally cancel Dance Land's permits and operating charter and technically the place was resuming its dance hall status. Even some of the yuppies from Settlement were suddenly interested in stopping by to take in some of the new style gyrations.

The Bliss City Council was caught completely off guard and threw itself into a flurry of ordinance creating to combat this evil interloper. Nobody had ever even dared to suggest opening such a den of inequity within the good Christian confines of Bliss's city limits, and a woeful lack of laws were on the books to stop it from happening. Thunderous denunciations reverberated throughout the houses of worship in Bliss as the city's considerable clergymen found a dastard cause to rally around.

The heat rained down upon Community Development and an army of inspectors were dispatched to nit-pick and fault find the hoochie coochie house of sin right out of business. Anticipating this course of panic, Dance Land's new owners promptly tied up their many violations in appeals courts while hiding behind grandfather status to keep their doors open. It was an ugly episode for Sheila Swift and the city attorney's office as they found themselves with their legal hands tied and the religious right condemning their lack of activity.

While the violations and accusations wound their way at a snail's pace through the court system, Dance Land's new owners became more brazen and embarked on expanding the operation throughout the whole building. The ultimate gesture of disregard for Bliss and its rules was the construction of a giant sign, shaped like the chrome babes found on truck driver's mud flaps, with flashing neon proclaiming the place "Cowpokes."

I could not in good conscience send Della and Sharon to inspect Cowpokes, but to build on the case against them and document their added violations routine inspections had to be made. It was decided that Red and I would go together to watch each other's backs.

On a warm and sunny Tuesday afternoon we pulled into Cowpokes' parking lot and found a space among a couple of dozen battered jalopies, a smattering of work trucks and several owner-operated big rigs. The lot was strewn with fast-food cartons and broken beer bottles. I recognized the stench of a surfacing septic system and a quick look behind the building confirmed my suspicions.

The building now housed three separate operations. The strip club was the largest and occupied the west end of the massive metal structure. The truck rental people had fled from the east side of the building which now housed a retail store that promised adult videos, games and more in fluorescent letters across blacked-out windows. In the center was a glass-swinging door labeled "Art Studios."

I looked at Red and asked, "So where do we start?"

Red clipped his Fire Marshal's badge and I.D. to his shirt pocket, pointed at the dance club and said, "Let's start with the jiggle queens." I put on my I.D., grabbed a clipboard and flashlight and followed.

We were stopped just inside the front door by a massive woman in a flowered muumuu with tattoos of men's anatomy on her arms and no front teeth. She was demanding a cover charge over the pounding bass of disco music. Red pointed at his badge and she waved us in with a slight bow.

It was dark and stank of beer-soaked carpet inside. On the large center stage a forty-something woman danced listlessly while attempting to cover generous amounts of cellulite on her ample rear and thighs with two small Japanese fans. A painfully thin girl with pale skin had attracted most of the meager crowd to her small platform on the right side of the dank room and was busy relieving her admirers of their folded dollars without the use of her hands. A tiny woman with teased hair who swayed from side to side and stared into space occupied a third platform near the bar on the left side of the room. These were definitely not coeds working their way through college.

Red turned toward me and yelled over the music, "Try not to get distracted." It was an easy command to follow.

A tall man with greasy hair and polyester pants and shirt

came crashing through the door by the center stage and rushed directly toward us. Yelling above the din in a surprisingly high-pitched voice he asked, "What can I do ya for?"

Red replied, "We're here to do the routine fire inspection. Is the manager or owner here?"

The man squeaked back, "I'm Rocko; I watch the place during the day. The manager doesn't come in 'til late and I don't even know who owns this joint."

Rocko wasn't the only one who could not pin down exact ownership of Cowpokes. Sheila Swift and her legal eagles had been hard at work with county and state attorneys attempting to sift through the maze of shill companies created to camouflage ultimate corporate responsibility for the carnal complex. Whenever a lackey, like Rocko, got arrested for stepping over the line another two-bit hoodlum would appear to take charge. Cowpokes accepted only cash, which was placed in big iron strongboxes for collection by some phantom at odd hours of the day. Cowpokes played a masterful game of ownership hide and seek.

Red walked past Rocko toward the door he had burst forth from and I was right behind him with Rocko in tow. Inside was a dressing room with several chairs in front of mirrors ringed by exposed light bulbs. Half a dozen women strolled around in various stages of nakedness, oblivious to our presence, waiting for their stage names to be called for duty at one of the platforms out front.

I made notes regarding the over-loading of electrical outlets with curling irons, hair dryers and shavers. There were missing breakers in the electrical panel and the rear doors had to be unlocked at the far end of a dark corridor with no lit exit sign. Rocko said, "Yes, Sir," and shook his head in agreement to everything Red noted for correction.

The strippers protested when Rocko unplugged the tools of their trade and made them move a rolling rack of tattered feather and lace garments that hid the fire extinguisher on the wall. We were back out front in the daylight and fresh air with a list of violations, the worst of which were corrected on the spot, in thirty minutes.

Red pointed to the far east end of the building and said, "Let's get the smut out of the way next. That so called "Art Studio" in the middle there is a new one on me and it looks spooky."

A bell rang at the top of the door and we made a sharp right turn and walked up a long ramp as soon as we entered the adult entertainment store. Lining the walls on both sides were leather and spike doohickeys designed to punish every part of the human anatomy and apparently cause great discomfort in various animals. Behind a glass counter full of adult toys, sitting on a metal stool, chain smoking and reading a copy of "Ho Baby" magazine was a person of questionable gender, dressed in black from head to toe, with purple spiked hair and numerous nose rings.

I tapped on the glass counter with my flashlight and said, "We're Bliss Fire Marshals and we're here to do the routine inspection."

The counter person replied, "So?" and never looked up from the magazine.

Red shook his head and said, "Let's get this done and get out of here."

I turned around to face the open store and involuntarily gasped, "Oh, my god!"

Dozens of racks stuffed with magazines emblazoned with pictures of people and animals having sex with each other were lined up at the entry to a large display area. Mixed-in with the appalling periodicals were shorter racks of corresponding videotapes. Hand-lettered signs hung from the ceiling above grouped sections labeled: Men on Women, Women on Women, Men on Men, and Other.

On the right wall near the middle of the room was an unlocked fire exit with a working sign above the door. We rolled a built-in fire hose out the door from a cabinet on the wall next to it, turned on the water and got nothing. Red made the note while I put the dead hose back in its case.

We walked through an open doorway at the back of the first room with "Peep Show" stenciled on a piece of cardboard above the frame. Inside the back room were ten small booths forming a half-circle that were barely large enough for the single plastic chairs that were inside each cubbyhole. Quarter-operated mechanisms in the cubbies raised a partition allowing the occupants to view a nude dancer on a small stage on the other side.

A stooped woman in a paisley duster was busy mopping the floors inside the cubicles and around their entry doors. I looked at Red and said, "Man, do these floors feel…"

Red held his hand up to stop me in mid sentence and said, "Don't even say it!"

At one end of the peep booths was a locked door. I stopped the mop lady from her chores and asked, "Do you have a key to this door."

She scowled at me and said, "Nobody goes in there but the girls!"

I shot back, "We're the Bliss Fire Marshals and unless you want us to shut this whole building down, I'd suggest you let us in there to finish our inspection."

The mop lady squinted at me and replied, "Well, why didn't

you say so? Do you have any idea how many perverts ask me to let them get at the ladies back there every day? She pulled a clump of keys from the front pocket of her housecoat and yelled over the partition, "Ladies, there's a couple of gentlemen coming back there to see ya."

A female voice shrieked and then yelled back, "Do they know what the rate is?"

The mop lady finished unlocking the door and yelled, "It's the Fire Marshals and I don't think that's what they're here for." She stood in front of the door fumbling with her keys to give the ladies in the back a little time to prepare for our arrival. We could hear them scurrying around, slamming doors and getting dressed before the mop lady let us pass.

The same female voice as before yelled, "Let 'em come, Hazel, we're decent."

Red and I walked in to find five young ladies in soiled silk bathrobes squeezed together on a tattered sofa just to the right of the small stage and out of sight from the peep booths. Four or five small rooms had been walled off creating a hallway to the rear exit, which had a chain and padlock dangling from the door's panic bar. Each room had a small refrigerator, cot and clothes locker with a curtain for a door.

I opened the back exit, which led directly into the sewage from the backed-up septic system. It would take a raging fire to force someone through that door and into the muck beyond.

Red stood firm by the door we had entered and pointed as he instructed me to, "Check the electrical panel on that wall over there."

I looked and the box was directly above and behind the sofa

where our dancers were nervously fidgeting. They began to elbow each other and giggle as I approached, but didn't offer to move. As I leaned over to open the metal door and inspect the breakers inside. I said, "Excuse me ladies, but I need to look inside this electrical panel."

One of the gals let out a harsh screech and clutched her flimsy robe tightly together at her chest. She bent over and turned away from me as if I was attempting to peer down her front. I recognized her voice as the same gal that had yelled at Hazel and was probably baring all her assets for twenty-five cents before we arrived. The rest of the girls roared with laughter as I rapidly backed away.

Still clutching her robe she said, "I don't care who you are, it still costs money to look at these, but if you want to come back when you have a little more time and cash, I'm sure we can work something out" This sent the other girls into hysterics and even Red was chuckling.

I felt my face burn red and stammered, "Thanks for the offer, but no thanks."

Red and I turned and left. I could still hear the girls laughing when they locked the door behind us. As we walked away the girl yelled one more time, "You'll be back, honey. I could see the sparks in your eyes."

We were back out front with one to go. I said, "Red, I don't think the last one could be any worse than that. Do you?"

Red shook his head and said, "It gets worse every time I come out here. I honestly don't know what to expect anymore. I do know that I'd better not hear of you coming back to take that girl up on her offer.

I laughed and said, "Don't worry. This place is creeping me out."

We both took a deep breath and strolled into the "Art Studio." A middle-aged lady in a red cat suit confronted us as soon as we cleared the door. The entry room was all mirrors and rates were etched into the glass on one wall defining charges by the half-hour. Cat Woman said, "Welcome, gentlemen," and pressed an intercom button on the wall by the rates.

A buzzer in the back summoned four young ladies dressed in very revealing lingerie who shuffled into the room in single file and lined up by Cat Woman. The girls struck different poses and froze. I just stood there and looked stupid.

Red said, "Umm, that's not why we're here."

Cat Woman replied, "Oh, really? Now don't be shy, you're among friends."

Red said, "No, ma'am. I'm the Fire Marshal and we're here to do your inspection."

Cat Woman pursed her lips and said, "Fine. You'll have to talk to Harry. He's in the back."

She shooed the girls out of the way and we followed her down a hall toward the rear of the building. There were four rooms with open doors along the left side of the hall. I looked into the open doorways as we passed and couldn't believe what I saw. The first was decorated like a cheap motel room. The second was done up to look like a kitchen. The third looked like a little girl's bedroom, but it was the fourth room that shocked me most. The fourth room had corrugated steel on the walls spray painted with lewd graffiti. Hanging over a bed in the center were two sets of furry handcuffs. There was one red light bulb dangling from the ceiling by a wire.

In the back room Harry sat behind a cheap desk watching soap operas on a tiny television. One armless sleeve of his plaid shirt was pinned to his shoulder and his only hand was resting on a chrome forty-five magnum. Next to the gun and bolted to the desk was a big steel box with a slot on top for depositing money.

Harry looked up when we came in the room and demanded, "What do you want?"

The Cat Woman said, "They're fire marshals and they want to inspect the place."

Harry grunted and went back to watching his television. The girls gathered on a large mattress in one corner of the room and began playing cards. The Cat Woman sat on the edge of Harry's desk and strummed her false nails while stroking Harry's matted head. I felt positive that nobody had ever shown up in this place with art supplies of any kind. Red and I gave the tight quarters a quick look and got the heck out of there. Nobody acknowledged our leaving.

We never slowed down outside the "Art Studio's" door and headed straight for Red's truck. Once inside and headed back to Bliss I turned to Red and said, "I feel like I need a long shower."

Red grinned and replied, "Man, we probably need to be sterilized or something."

It turned out that Cowpokes had picked the wrong part of the Bible belt to set up a sleaze shop. Profits never justified the money that was being spent on the place and the constant employee arrests were taking a toll on operations. The initial curiosity of Cowpokes' customers wore away rapidly.

Three weeks after Red and I made our jittery fire inspection, the strip club at Cowpokes mysteriously caught fire. The damage was extensive, but nobody got hurt. The investigation never revealed an exact cause for the fire, but arson was at the top of the betting pool list.

Another army of inspectors descended on Cowpokes and deemed the whole building structurally unsound. There was no red tape to slow down the demolition of the site, and the place was razed in record time. Cowpokes bit the dust, and the people of Bliss could not have been happier about its demise.

Shoveling piles of money into an incinerator would be the only way to burn through heaps of cash faster and have less to show when its gone than paying for a fireworks show.

CHAPTER 25
JULY FOURTH
◆◆◆

Fire Marshals loathe the Fourth of July! The celebration of our nation's independence occurs during the hottest, driest and often windiest month of the year. A heightened sense of patriotism coupled with readily available pyrotechnics creates a perfect environment for accidental fires. All across our fair nation people attempt to burn their homes, their neighborhoods, fields, forests and businesses with their own personal fireworks shows.

Larger cities and towns ban the sale and ownership of fireworks in a vain attempt to keep people from shooting fireballs onto roofs and into fields of bone-dry grass, while giant fireworks stands are set up just outside their city limit lines to supply pyromaniacs with the tools of their trade. A glowing punk and a sack of tiny rocket propelled explosives in the hands of an alcohol-fueled reveler is the perfect mix for a fire related disaster.

Every year fingers will be blown off, eyes put out and property lost to the careless use of fireworks, but it's an American tradition that's not about to go away. Charged with halting the ballistic ballyhoo is the local fire marshal. While the rest of America is celebrating, fire marshals across the land are attempting to keep merry citizens from maiming themselves or burning up their property.

In the ultimate act of "Do as I say, not as I do" many cities outlaw the ownership and use of personal fireworks and then invite their populace to a giant fireworks extravaganza funded by tax dollars. The logic behind this maneuver seems to be that starting a massive conflagration in one location with thousands of people and vehicles on hand would be easier to manage than hundreds of tiny fires spread all over town. Spectators at large fireworks shows are often impassioned by the grandeur of it all and can't wait to get home and shoot off their own stash of firecrackers and bottle rockets.

The true sign that any city has become too flush with tax dollars is the decision to put on fireworks displays. Shoveling piles of money into an incinerator would be the only way to burn through heaps of cash faster and have less to show when its gone than paying for a fireworks show. Not only are the pyrotechnics themselves incredibly expensive, but the city will have to supply extra police for crowd control, extra fire fighters in case the show gets out of hand and every person in fire prevention will be on duty to stop the spectators from adding their own personal touches to the event.

The first fireworks displays in Bliss were launched off of the Bliss Lake dam. This made great sense from a fire prevention standpoint. The molten flack from spent shells would fall harmlessly into the lake, unless they rained down on some unfortunate boat, which would still be safely contained even if it burst into flame. But not everyone had a boat and only a two-lane road provided access to the park nearest the dam so viewers of the show felt left out or trapped when the show ended.

The City Council and Bliss's most vocal business leaders huddled together to solve the venue problem. It was decided that a large parking lot for the gathering of the masses was needed, and a wide-open space would be good so the fireworks could be seen for miles. The Council's focus turned toward the open fields south of the Horizon Hills mall. Red argued that increasing the possibility of burning down the city's largest revenue generator was not wise, but his concerns went unheeded.

When I attended my first Bliss fireworks show as the Assistant Fire Marshal, it was in its third year at the mall location. A couple of restaurants and a motel had been constructed near the launch site to add to the suspense of a possible fire outbreak. The property owner had mowed chest-deep weeds where the flatbed trailer holding the mortars for launching the fireworks would be parked leaving rows of tinder-dry grass underfoot.

We had managed to position the launching pad far enough away from the crowds and buildings to meet the minimum requirements of the National Fire Code, but a blustery south wind was threatening to blow spent shells straight into the crowds that would be gathered in the parking lots surrounding the mall. Throughout the day of the fourth, winds gusted near forty miles per hour.

The show would begin after dark on Saturday. Red gathered me, Sharon, Della and Spoons together on Friday to go over our game plan. We were in a small meeting room and Red said grumpily, "Everyone is expected to be at the mall by 7:00 PM Saturday. There will be no exceptions. Be sure to take home your I.D.s, flashlights and two-way radios. We'll meet at the launching trailer and fan out from there."

We were all loitering around the flatbed trailer wondering where Red was when he called on the radio, "Fire Marshal Two, I'm at the top of the hill trying to clear people out of the fire lane. Have Spoons stay by the trailer to give the operator the go ahead to start the show when I call him on the radio and you and the girls come up here and help with the crowd."

I replied, "Roger that. We'll be right up there."

There were thousands of cars and people in the parking lot jockeying for the best viewing positions. People on blankets in the grass medians between the parking lot and the mall's ring road had been holding their spots since late afternoon. Kids were running everywhere and the scene was one of mild pandemonium. I found Red trying to clear parked cars and people in lawn chairs out of the fire lanes that circled near the mall's main buildings. If there were a fire or a medical emergency, it would be the only way to get equipment in and out of the swarm.

Red spotted me and yelled, "Help me get these people out of the fire lane. It's getting late and we have to have it cleared before we can start the show."

I started by approaching a man sitting on top of a rusty van. His group had spread out in lawn chairs around the van and they were blocking the entire fire lane. I yelled up at him, "Hey, you can't park here, you'll have to move."

He looked down with bloodshot eyes and a beer in one hand and yelled back, "Says who?"

I replied, "I'm the fire marshal and I say you have to move

this van and your group out of the fire lane."

The man shook his head and shot back. "I ain't goin' anywhere. The show's about to start and it's too late to get a good spot."

I tried to reason with him, but he looked away as if I would give up and leave. The people parked safely outside the fire lane began to take an interest in our confrontation. I decided to get them involved and yelled at the man on the van, "Listen. I am the guy who says when this fireworks show is going to start and I'm not starting it until you get this van and these people out of my fire lane."

A guy from the crowd yelled, "Hey, buddy. You're holding up the show."

A lady chimed in, "We're all waiting on you. Why don't you do what the man said?"

A group of men piled out of a camouflage painted pickup truck and began walking toward the van. I figured it was about to get ugly, so I played my trump card, "Listen, mister. If you don't move I'll have to radio for some policemen to come and arrest you and have your van towed away. Why don't you make it easy on yourself and just leave?"

The mention of policemen threw an immediate scare into him and he bolted down from the van, climbed inside and started it up. The rest of his group picked up their chairs and filtered into the crowd. The vigilante brigade from the camouflage truck turned back as the van man drove away.

I turned around and there stood Red with a big grin. He said, "Ryan, you've got to get it done faster, but that wasn't bad. Don't wait to take the gloves off with these people or they'll eat you alive."

It was now dusk and Red and I walked to the far south end of the parking lot where we could look down on the launch trailer. The wind was still gusting, but the gales were coming fewer and farther apart. Red got on the radio to tell Spoons to have the technician fire off a test round so we could gauge the wind's effect on it. Spoons didn't answer. We both scanned the area below in the dim light and could just make Spoons out about fifty yards from the trailer talking to a group of firefighters milling around their truck.

Red called on the radio again and we could see one of the firefighters tap Spoons on the shoulder and point at his radio.

A few seconds later Spoons answered, "This is inspector 3, go ahead."

Red shot back, "What are you doing over there and why didn't you answer my calls?"

There was a pregnant pause and Spoons crackled back over the air, "I forgot to turn on my radio."

I knew Della and Sharon were listening to this conversation and loving every minute. Red instructed Spoons to have the technician fire a test mortar and in minutes a single streak of light lifted from the trailer to a small explosion in the sky. The crowd roared anticipating the start of the show and we watched as the flack from the shell sailed into the mall's ring road.

Red turned to me and said, "That's not good."

I knew he was right, but there were fifty thousand people waiting for us to get this show on the road and the pressure was intense. We waited and waited and the crowd got louder and nastier by the minute.

Finally there was a lull in the wind and Red said, "Well, Ryan, it's do or die." He keyed his radio and instructed Spoons,

"Tell the technician to start the show, but keep close in case the wind gets wild and we have to stop."

In moments the night sky began to light up in brilliant colors and the applause and cheers from the crowd punctuated the echoing explosions that thundered across the parking lot. I had allowed myself to get caught up in staring at the sky when Red nudged me in the arm and said, "Do you think we ought to tell the fire boys to put that blaze under their truck out?"

I looked down to see a small fire growing in the dry grass under the fire truck that had been parked near the launch trailer. A piece of smoldering flack had floated under the truck, and the firefighters were staring up at the sky watching the show and never noticed.

Red called on the radio, "Truck seven, you guys might want to put out that fire under your rig there."

One of the firefighters spun around and then all six of them sprang into action. They quickly extinguished the rapidly growing fire and hardly anyone else noticed as the collective gaze of the masses was focused skyward.

The wind piped up a little and glowing embers began to fall closer to the parking lot where Red and I were standing. Then a large piece of molten shell landed next to a family sitting twenty feet from us and set the grass on fire. The mother of the group just sat and stared at the growing blaze while Red and I rushed over and stomped it out. The lady turned her head back to the show in the sky when we were done as if that had been a planned part of the experience.

The explosions were getting bigger and coming closer together as the show began to peak, and now large chunks of fiery mortar shells were crashing into the parking lot and busting into embers. Red yelled, "Ryan, we've got to stomp out as many of those as we can!"

I said, "Won't they just burn themselves out on the asphalt?"

Red said, "Maybe, but what if one of those cars in the parking lot has a gas leak?"

We both scampered up the hill and spent the next ten minutes chasing down skidding embers and stomping out smoldering flack. There was a slight pause in the action and I heard a massive mortar fire. It seemed like forever before it exploded and released what looked like burning Chinese lanterns into the air. I looked at Red, he turned to stare at me and both of our mouths dropped wide open. The explosions continued, but the lanterns floated on the wind and disappeared over the outer walls right on top of the mall.

Red said, "What the heck were those? There was no mention of floating lanterns in the permit application."

The fireworks finale began and all Red and I could do was stare at the top of the mall waiting for the signs of our career-ending fire to break out. The reflections of massive explosions bounced off the mall's walls and the largest of the mortars boomed behind us, and we still stared in disbelief at where the flaming lanterns had sailed out of sight. When the explosions ended and the crowd went wild cheering we remained transfixed on the mall's roof.

The next morning in Billy Belcher's staff meeting everyone congratulated Red on what a splendid job he'd done pulling off the fireworks show without a hitch. Billy announced that the Fire Chief himself had been on top of the mall watching with management, friends and family and he had nothing but praise for how we had handled the situation and made it look so effortless.

Red and I had somehow gone completely unnoticed while we ran about stomping out fires. No mention was made of the surprise flaming lanterns that had floated on top of the mall. The newspaper had called the fireworks show, "…a fun and relaxing spectacle for all…" I'm sure it was for everyone but the fire marshals, who have always dreaded July Fourth fireworks celebrations.

I slinked home from my office for the solace of my bed in hopes that I might quietly pass away there and thus escape my misery.

CHAPTER 26
SICK DAY
◆◆◆

I was reared to revere a strong Christian work ethic that resulted in my forming some sort of misguided belief that I should never miss work due to illness. For ten years I dragged myself to work when I should have been home in bed to preserve my spotless record of never having taken a sick day off. This feat impressed nobody but me when I would point it out to fellow employees.

Jocko used to say, "Ryan, everyone needs to take a sick day now and then, even if it's for their own mental health." He practiced what he preached and never once carried over a sick day from one year to the next.

Most of Bliss city employees viewed sick days as vacation and used them accordingly. Should the end of the year approach with sick days on the books they were certain to contract some illness that would keep them away from work.

Another major motivator for my not staying home during the workweek was daytime television. I have been too sick to read or write and too congested to sleep, but I have never been so indisposed that I could stand to watch daytime television. Evidently advertisers believe that only people who need jobs learning to drive big rigs or assistance with suing for personal loss or injury are home during weekdays. These same viewers must also be enamored with the sordid doings of actors and actresses who are not quite ready for movie roles or prime-time appearances.

Shortly after my tenth anniversary working for the city I contracted influenza. It was not a garden-variety inconvenience, but the devil's own malady and I was an aching, snot-producing mess when Red discovered me cowering in my office on a Monday morning.

Red stopped short at my door and said, "My god, Ryan, you look like death!"

I sniffled back, "I feel much worse than I look. If it were not for the drugs propping me up, I would surely be in a fetal position on the floor."

Red took a half step back and said, "I know you have a weird preoccupation with never taking a sick day, but I don't want to catch what you have and I don't want you giving it to any of my staff. You gather yourself up, go home and stay there until you get over your crud. I mean it."

I was too weak to argue. My perfect attendance record was going down for the count and so was I. I slinked home from my office for the solace of my bed in hopes that I might quietly pass away there and thus escape my misery. Death would surely be a welcome respite from my respiratory wretchedness.

I was now living in a two-bedroom, two-bath town home on the southwest side of Bliss. As property got scarcer and pricier some diabolical developer had come up with the concept of using zero lot lines for home construction. One entire side of a home would be built of brick, with no windows or openings, so it could be erected directly on its lot line and then the adjacent structure placed just far enough away to meet the building code requirements for a proper separation to create a firebreak. The result was row after row of tightly packed and inexpensive houses with lawns the size of bed sheets.

Aching and delirious I crawled into bed and had just gotten still when the beagle next door began to bawl the call to the hunt. The window at the head of my bed was in the rear corner of the house placing me eight feet from the fence that contained the wailing beast on the opposite side. I had been subjected to this monster's howling on many prior occasions, but today he was as close to top form as I was to imminent death. For hours he bayed and seemingly never let up for even a short breath. It was a remarkable tour de force and there were no signs of him tiring.

I dragged myself out of bed and retrieved the cordless phone to call next door in hopes that someone would be there to quell the debilitating din. No such luck. I lay in bed and listened to the cheerful greeting on their answering machine and at the sound of the tone laid my receiver on my windowsill to share the cacophony at length.

Sometime after five I began to hear the car doors of people returning home from their various jobs. A short time later the barking stopped. The loony lady next door must have taken her dog inside. For the first time all day there was peace and I began to slowly fade away.

With the briefest of nods to the sandman, I was jolted awake by a knock at my front door. I attempted to ignore this intrusion, but a second round of knocking that was much longer and more persistent ensued. I crept out of bed, put on a robe and slunk to the door where a quick look through the peephole revealed an agitated looking policeman on the other side.

I opened the door and Officer Gantry cut right to the chase, "Mr. Ryan, did you call and leave a message on your neighbor's answering machine?"

I was having a little trouble focusing on him so I said, "Yes, I did, but would you mind coming inside so I can sit while we talk. I'm not feeling very well."

Officer Gantry followed me inside and shut the door behind us as I slumped onto the sofa. He towered above me and scanned his clipboard while he filled me in on the reason for his visit, "The female complainant next door reported that you called and filled an entire two-hour tape on her answering machine with what sounds like a dog howling. Is that true?"

I said, "Yes, I suppose it is."

Office Gantry continued, "She stated that she feels threatened by your actions and that constitutes phone harassment."

I know there was a look of puzzlement on my face when I asked, "Did you listen to the tape?"

Officer Gantry replied, "She played it for me and she also said that it sounds like her dog."

My mouth involuntarily dropped open and it took me a minute to respond, "Are you telling me that I threatened her with the incessant baying of her own dog?"

Officer Gantry shook his head while he explained, "It doesn't matter what you put on that tape, if she feels threatened by it, then it's phone harassment."

I rubbed my eyes and tried to explain, "Look, I work for the city and I came home sick with the flu. All I wanted to do was lie in bed and suffer quietly when her dog started up and wouldn't quit. When I called to ask for help and got their machine, I put my receiver on my window and left it there so they could see how incredibly obnoxious that beagle was all day."

Officer Gantry shot back, "I don't care. If you've got a dog problem call Critter Control. Don't call this lady again. She's a psycho and she's going to get you into trouble. We get late night paranoid calls from her all the time."

I was still for a minute and asked, "Is that it?"

Officer Gantry said, "Yeah, but you really should go back to bed. You look like death. I'll let myself out."

I crawled back to bed and slipped into a welcome coma. I didn't make it back to work all week, and the beagle must have been cooped up inside because it didn't bother me.

A full month slipped by without the beagle barking, but I knew it was too good to be true. It was around midnight on a Tuesday when the beagle began to bay nonstop and by three in the morning I couldn't take it anymore.

I knew better than to call next door and I didn't want to disturb any of the Critter Control officers at such an ungodly hour, so I got dressed and went outside to pay my neighbors a visit. It looked like every light in their house was lit and I knocked on the door. The porch light came on and I could see an eye peer at me through the peephole so I waved hello, but the door never opened. I knocked again and the eye disappeared.

I stood on the neighbor's porch for several minutes waiting

while the beagle continued to wail at the night. Finally I gave up and went back to bed. I had not been between the sheets for more than ten minutes when I heard the slam of car doors in the street in front of my house. It hit me instantly. She called the cops on me again.

I got dressed and went outside. Two policemen were searching the bushes on each side of my neighbor's house with flashlights. I walked over to them and said, "I'm pretty sure you're looking for me."

The officer nearest me said, "What?" He could not hear what I'd said because the barking beagle was several feet from him on the other side of the front fence howling away.

I yelled above the yowling, "I think you are looking for me!"

The front door opened and the loony lady peeked outside. The second officer stepped up on the porch to talk to her and the first officer and I joined him. She pointed at me and shrieked, "That's him!"

The second officer turned to face me and I yelled, "Hello again, Officer Gantry."

Officer Gantry attempted to speak to me, but I could not hear what he was saying over the dog's barking. He turned to the lady peeking from behind her front door and yelled, "Would you please stop that dog from barking!"

The door slammed closed and the officers and I stood on her porch and looked at each other. The sound of the dog's baying left the front of the house and went toward the rear. When the lady cracked her door open again the dog was still barking, but the sound was muffled as if it was locked in a closed room in the rear of her home.

Officer Gantry said, "Is this the man that was peeking in your windows, ma'am?"

The loony lady stammered, "I'm not sure."

I said, "Look, lady, you've gone too far now. You know all I did was knock on your door and wait here on your porch. I saw you look at me though the peephole. All I wanted to do is get you to stop your beagle from barking."

The loony lady said, "I'm tired. I'm going to bed." She slammed the door shut and it sounded like no fewer than six locks were chained and bolted before the porch light went out. I couldn't help laughing out loud.

Officer Gantry looked at me, but was not amused. He said, "I thought I told you to call Critter Control if you had any more dog trouble?"

I straightened up and said, "I didn't want to have to drag any of those guys out here at this time of the morning. That dog's been at it since midnight and all I did was come over and knock on the door to try and talk to them. The house was all lit up so I figured they were awake."

Officer Gantry said, "That lady is going to get you locked up if you're not careful. If I were you I'd go down to the police station and file a report telling your side of the story first thing in the morning. You'd better have something on the record besides these wild complaints she's been filing on you."

I said, "Yes, sir. I'll do just that."

The two officers got in their squad car and sat with the interior light on filling out reports. I went back to bed. The clock on my nightstand read 4:00 AM. That beagle was really starting to bug me.

My ketch was named "No Tan Lines" in honor of the
ladies who crewed in club races for me and she was to be
my future escape dreamboat when I retired from Bliss.

CHAPTER 27
MY SHIP CAME IN

The Bliss Civic Center began to swell with employees and overflow with records to the point that storage rooms and mop closets were being eyed for conversions into staff habitat. Rex and Jocko now had four health inspectors and three code enforcement officers. Gene Autrey had an assistant and six building inspectors. Red had me and I attempted to smooth the feathers ruffled by three fire inspectors during the course of their duties. That was just the crowding that occurred on our side of the second floor and it was even tighter across the hall where building plans were piled like bunkers and overflowed from cabinets that surrounded engineers and their field inspectors.

The lack of available space was just as great among the offices downstairs as the City of Bliss and its employee count were showing no signs of abating their phenomenal growth. The annual city picnic was beginning to look more like an army bivouac than an intimate gathering of personnel.

I had ever so slowly climbed from the bottom ranks as a

humble health inspector to a job in city management with a realistic shot at advancement within the foreseeable future. I wasn't going to get wealthy working for the city, but a single guy with no debt could live comfortably on what I made and begin to forge some future dreams if I didn't miff too many muckamucks along the way.

I did manage to irritate Dick Darling by foolishly signing a petition to ban smoking in all public buildings without considering the political consequences of my actions. It irked him to no end when the proposition passed, and he made it a point to memorize every employee who had dared pen their name on the antismoking proposal and glowered at them whenever they crossed paths. Ironically it became my job as Assistant Fire Marshal to enforce the no smoking ordinance, which Dick blatantly ignored by puffing away in his office and ducking into closets and meeting rooms around the Civic Center to indulge his habit. I never considered citing him for his constant violations.

I had not only improved my working and housing arrangements, but the little boat that we had terrorized the polyester-clad ladies at The Angler's Hideaway years ago was sold and a thirty-five-foot ketch was procured as its replacement. There are basically two types of boaters to be found on marina docks; power boaters who realize the restrictions placed on them by having to drive from marina to marina to replenish their fuel and plug into shore power at the end of each day, and sailors who all seem to harbor deep down the dream of someday chucking everything and sailing across oceans on their ideal boat.

My ketch was named *"No Tan Lines"* in honor of the ladies who crewed in club races for me and she was to be my future escape dreamboat when I retired from Bliss.

I even forsook the time honored Texas tradition of driving a pickup truck and bought myself a new sports car. Yup, things were looking pretty good.

The one constant that remained throughout my ten-year career with Bliss was dating Denise. Denise was smart, good looking, had a promising career with a giant telecommunications corporation and an independent nature that I found to be most intriguing. We never lived together and she owned a house in a tiny north Texas hamlet that was far enough away to make trading weekend visits a real treat while creating a separation that deterred us from over imposing on each other's lives during the workweek. We both agreed that it was a sweet set-up.

Denise and I vacationed together. We traveled to the mountains to ski, visited mutual friends in cities all over the world and chartered cruising sailboats in the islands. Our favorite destinations began to be those of a tropical nature so it was not too huge a surprise when she came to me one day with news of a possible work relocation with her company.

We were at my house in Bliss when Denise said, "I'm pretty sure that I am in line for a job with our corporate offices in Florida. If they want me, I plan to move as soon as possible. What do you think about that?"

I had never considered the fact that I might someday lose this woman, but I wanted the best for her in all things so I replied, "I think that would be great for your career."

Denise smiled and asked, "Would you come with me?"

I tried to be realistic about the situation and stoically replied, "I wouldn't have a job out there and I haven't done anything but work for a city for the last ten years. I'm vested in the city's retirement program and could pack it in at a young age if I stay."

Denise's smile never wavered as she made me an impossible to refuse offer, "You don't have to work right away. Quit your job, bring your boat and let's move to south Florida. We can make it on what I'll earn until you get your new situation figured out."

I must have looked shocked and surprised because Denise was laughing when I shouted, "Then it's a no brainer. Let's move to Florida!"

Denise threw her arms around me and I was sure I'd made the right decision. I opened a bottle of champagne while Denise put Gloria Estafan's "Greatest Hits" CD into my stereo and cranked up the volume as high as it would go. We were dancing and toasting each other to the raucous strains of the Latin dance song "*Conga*" when I thought I heard the doorbell.

I went to the door and looked through the peephole. There stood a frowning Officer Gantry. I opened the door, champagne in hand, toasted toward him, took a big gulp of my wine and bowed with a flourish. Officer Gantry's frown grew more menacing.

Denise had looked around the corner, saw me with Officer Gantry and turned the music down. Gloria was now insisting that the "*Rhythm Is Gonna Get You*" but at a much more subtle sound level.

Officer Gantry said, "I'm sure you can guess why I'm here."

I took another little sip of bubbly and replied, "Let's see. Could it be that the Loony Lady next door is not a Gloria Estefan fan?"

Officer Gantry cracked a wry little smile and said, "Why must you torture her and cause me so many headaches?"

Beaming with a champagne-induced grin I gushed my good news, "Officer Gantry, as far as I am concerned your problems here are over. I am moving to Florida in two weeks and I promise you I will attempt to be on my best behavior and not cause you any more grief as the result of spats between me and my crazy neighbor."

Officer Gantry's mouth gaped open. He didn't look convinced when he asked, "Are you for real?"

I promptly replied, "Yes! I'm out of here and out of your hair forever."

Officer Gantry stuck his hand out and while shaking mine said, "Mr. Ryan, I'm happy for you. I can't say that I'm sorry to see you go, but I wish you the best of luck."

Officer Gantry wheeled around and almost skipped back to his squad car. I walked outside far enough to look around the front of my house next door and caught the Loony Lady eyeballing my house from her front porch. I gave her a sweeping wave with a dramatic bow, which sent her scurrying inside followed by a flourish of deadbolts and chains being thrashed into their locking positions.

I went back inside to find Denise siphoning off the last of the champagne. She asked, "Is everything OK?"

I replied, "It couldn't be better," and we continued dancing with Gloria, but utilized a much lower volume, which was punctuated by a beagle baying in the background.

City employees are notorious for complaining about their jobs. Every fellow worker I knew was counting the days when they would no longer have to work for the city. Most would never be able to find the pay and benefits they enjoyed working in city government by laboring somewhere else so they were content to lament their lot and determined to hang on until retirement.

I strolled into Red's office the day after Denise had confirmed her new position in Florida, handed him two neatly typed paragraphs and said, "Here's my resignation."

Without reading it Red tossed the paper back at me and said, "Yeah, yeah, we all hate it here. I'm busy, don't bother me."

I handed my two-week notice back to him and said, "No, really. You'd better read that. I'm turning in my notice."

Red stopped working on his city ordinance variance, which was expected at the next council meeting and read my note. He looked up with a grin, sure that I was up to something and asked, "Is this for real?"

I smiled broadly and replied, "It sure is. Denise is getting transferred to south Florida and I'm going with her."

Red shook his head, reread my note and said, "You're kidding me?"

I said, "Nope! I'm out of here. There really is life outside of Bliss."

Red motioned toward a chair in front of his desk and said, "Sit down a minute." I did and we talked at length about my newly formed plans. Red had met Denise and liked her, but he was convinced that she would dump me when we moved in together in Florida.

He could not believe that I was just up and quitting a career that I'd invested over ten years in the making. He advised me to take more time in making this wild decision, and I assured him that my mind was made up and I was seizing this opportunity.

Word spread fast throughout the city and I began to make the rounds to say goodbye to all the friends I'd made. Some were sure that I was making a huge mistake, but most were excited about my future possibilities and a few even begged me to take them along.

When I got around to Barney Belcher all he could say was, "My god, Ryan, personnel says I'm going to have to pay you for all those sick days you never took and it's going to wreck my budget."

On my last day at Bliss I wore a straw hat and a Hawaiian shirt to work. I stopped downstairs in the main offices to say goodbye to the Assistant City Manager, Clyde Regal and he made me go into Dick Darling's office before I left. Dick looked up from a pile of papers on his desk and an ever-present cigarette smoldered in the ashtray by his side. Dick said, "Ryan, I can't say that I'm crushed to see you go, but I've had worse employees."

It turned out that Denise and I had purchased a condo in the same town that Dick had left to take the job as city manager in Bliss. He gave me the names of some of his favorite strip clubs near my new home and we parted with mutual nods and an awkward silence. We weren't going to miss each other, but I think he missed south Florida.

Red and the fire inspectors took me out for breakfast on my last day. We checked the most recent scores with the health inspectors and decided on The Pancake Hut. They gave me a coffee mug with their pictures on it and a beautiful ship's clock. As with most everyone I knew at the city, they had been wonderful to work alongside.

Red taped my resignation to the inside of the glass wall that faced the floor full of inspectors on the second level of the Civic Center. It said: This is a formal resignation from Ross Ryan to the City of Bliss. I am hereby filing a two-week notice of my intention to resign my position as the Bliss Assistant Fire Marshal. It has been a pleasure to work with you all. My ship has come in and it's docking on the east coast.

EPILOGUE

Ross and Denise bought a two-bedroom condominium off the New River in Fort Lauderdale, Florida with a sixty-five foot boat dock located a dozen steps out their back door. Denise was moving from a three-bedroom house and Ross from a two-bedroom townhouse so some drastic reductions in home furnishings were needed to downsize their possessions to fit within the confines of their new home.

Ross and Denise agreed to hold a mutual garage sale to eliminate redundant and unwanted household possessions. Much to his surprise, everything Ross owned was sold or donated to the needy. Ross had spent his entire bachelorhood accumulating a mismatched houseful of family castoffs and bargain acquisitions, which were suddenly deemed unsuitable. The new condo was tastefully decorated with Denise's carefully matched furniture sets, wall hangings and assorted dust collectors.

Denise's new job was focused entirely outside of the United States. She was now working with employees from Central America, South America and the Caribbean. She vastly broadened her people interaction skills and made countless new friends who introduced her and Ross to Latin American culture. Denise became a master at mixing business with pleasure on her corporate financed excursions south of the U.S. border.

Ross spent several months laboring to transform "*No Tan Lines*" from an inland-lake boat to a seafaring vessel. The sturdy ketch became an intrepid craft, which ferried Ross and Denise across the Atlantic to exotic ports in the Bahamas and the Florida Keys.

Ross attended the Maritime Professional Training School in Fort Lauderdale in pursuit of his captain's license. He graduated with flying colors, amassed the required hours of sea time and aced the Coast Guard's tests. With his Master's License Captain Ross began driving other people's yachts for a living. Ranging from the northeast coast of the United States to Trinidad, South America, Ross delivered yachts to ports where their owners wanted to play on them without spending their vacation time on long passages. The good captain also acted as chauffeur for rich yacht owners on day charters who entertained lavishly, partied hard and didn't want to be bothered with the responsibility of driving their own boats or putting them away at day's end.

After eleven years of dating in Texas and finally moving in together, Ross and Denise decided to get married. Denise wanted to get married on the beach, which made Ross very happy because they lived minutes away from the shoreline. Alas, the Atlantic coast would not do for the new bride and the pair jetted halfway around the world to tie the knot on the beach in Maui. It was a harbinger of the exciting travels and adventures that lay ahead for the happy couple.